Vol I

GENESIS

101 Shades of Clay

Vol I Genesis

©2022 by Catherine Elizabeth Clay

May 7th, 2022

ISBN: (Paperback)   979-8-88615-031-5

        (E-book)   979-8-88615-032-2

Inks and Bindings
888-290-5218
www.inksandbindings.com
orders@inksandbindings.com

CONTENTS

Dearly Beloved 19

In the Beginning... 31

The Gentle Art of Female Ejaculation
AKA How to Fuck Like a Porn Star 35

I TOUCH MYSELF 57

Awakenings..63

My First Crush 71

Rape 79

My First Lust 89

Don't Stand So Close to Me 95

My 1st Kisses 101

My first BJ..111

I had the Time of My Life 117

Like a Virgin...119

Melissa 125

Handy Dandy Andy 133

Superman...139

Tarkovsky...143

Vlad the Impaler 149

The Pilot 155

Русалка (Mermaid) 163

Andrei 167

Venice..171

Whip It Good 175

Jacinta...179

Zack...181

London Calling 185

Slap My Bitch Up My First Personal Rape 191

Ninja Pussy 203

Good Lovin'...207

Take My Breath Away 211

OCD 217

Cabrini Green 221

Anaïs NIИ 225

Battle of the Sexes 229

Monday December 13, 1999 233

Whiskey Dick...237

Seperate Bedrooms 239

About The Author..243

**"Say my name
Say my name
If nobody's around you
Say, 'Breonna I love you'" ~Destiny's Child**

Breonna

As one of the incidents to ignite the flame of all of the pain racism (we're all simply the human race) has been marring our lives far too long will go down as the darkest part of our history as people EVERYWHERE are being **W**oke.

In case you haven't figured out you will always be a single mother when you choose to have that child. Know that as A FACT. No time off for good behavior and if you're scum enough to drop them like kiddies at the pool then we, as a society, need to look at ourselves and realize birth isn't an answer to birth control and if you bitch about abortion then find another hate crime to start bitching about. Put on the **Elbow Grease** as we get strapped on and take you to new heights. "Oh... you don't want to have sex? But I want to fuck you up the ass to celebrate your promotion. Take one for the team. There is no I in team (yes there is in the font the smart-ass made it in)."

I'd like to give so many props to African American women who paved the way for white women like me. You were the first single moms that taught us we can and have to be a"**sister doing it for herself"~Eurythmics** now."

My 48th birthday, June 1st, was literally a RIOT! (my 49th present from my father was the Courier Journal article "**A day in the Life**" of the **Kingpin of Kentuckiana** [you ALL drank the kool-aid, m'kay?] so I'm repaying the "flavor" by singing, "Ding Dong the Witch is **DEAD**" because I honestly thought Halloween could not be a better holiday **UNTIL** my wicked step monster died on fucking Halloween!!!). A block party I could not join because I was not healthy enough to beat down the man. Like I'm trying to against the man who created me. I curled up in a ball that day with nothing to say and cried because of how Louisville lied. To yourselves the MOST. I knew daddy would shine in this case but not for the other race (there's only one race... the huMAN [Noone took the man from woman] race) but from the way he raised me I could hear him cheer "Hooray! Here's a new case FOR ME today!" If you had any idea... Or at least that was the prick I was raised by. **And after 50 years being like that I don't think he's changed in the last 20. 77... he's who he is down to the Core of his being and the marrow of his bones,"THE MAN"** from **"THE FAMILY"** (even deeper than Netflix because you don't expect a man with a family history mandating laws [him in sexual harassment] end up being a Kingpin. And knocking up a secretary. Tsk... homewreckers a different time indeed!) that made this country who she tiz today.

If I'm willing to show you my cunt why would I lie about HIM? He beat all the lies I could want to muster, impossible to follow through and I've been told it's a "character flaw" because I'm TOO honest. 🙄

So I write out her name and try to find the words that will rhythm throughout time as we walk together hand in hand because she ran out of luck and I actually **GIVE A FEW FLYING FUCKS**. Our names going down together in history with only one degree separating us with so many mysteries. My last name with yours converging our lifetime tours. Mine a little longer but yours is so much stronger.

Breonna probably never danced naked to Madonna
Breonna was too hot to sit in a sauna
Breonna had no time to go to **Henry's Farm** to pet a llama
Breonna's different smiles punctuated her face with bright commas
Breonna never joined a gang because she didn't wanna
Breonna broke it off with a man she found to be a conner
Breonna could still hear everyone in a channa
Breonna had to meet up with racist bwanas
Breonna never got to fly to Botswana
Breonna never got to eat food of Ghana
Breonna also never had plans to see Guyana
Breonna's probably didn't know about the actress Lana
Breonna had very few friends named Donna
Breonna never held a baby and introduced her to her monna :(---
Breonna couldn't imagine a life without her momma
Momma has to grow old without her beautiful baby girl, Breonna

I cannot tell you how sorry I am from the depths of my soul because I miss my mother every day. I couldn't imagine what it would have been like to have lost my sister when she had leukemia and my father wasn't around because we chose to live with our momma.

I feel that pain all the same just not as intimately as her own mother. Compounded infinitely by the sin of my father. So I say it loud and proud trying to fight back at the tyranny that made me me in his image yet denys not ONLY ME (his double entendre Tom boy son) but WHO continues the branch of Lt Colonel Thomas Eugene Clay, Sr.,Esquire's.

GOD DAMN MOTHER FUCKING ПЗДЕТЦ CLAY
DYNASTY. He's never met Cassius.
    **FUCK YOU FOR DENYING JUSTICE. NOW TAKE IT
LEICA A Man FROM YOUR BOY, Daddy.**

Breonna Breonna Breonna Breonna Breonna Breonna
Breonna Breonna Breonna Breonna Breonna Breonna
Breonna Breonna Breonna Breonna Breonna Breonna
Breonna Breonna Breonna Breonna Breonna Breonna
Breonna Breonna Breonna Breonna Breonna Breonna
Breonna Breonna Breonna Breonna Breonna Breonna
Breonna Breonna Breonna Breonna Breonna Breonna
Breonna Breonna Breonna Breonna Breonna Breonna
Breonna Breonna Breonna Breonna Breonna Breonna
Breonna Breonna Breonna Breonna Breonna Breonna
Breonna Breonna Breonna Breonna Breonna Breonna
Breonna Breonna Breonna Breonna Breonna Breonna
Breonna Breonna Breonna Breonna Breonna Breonna
Breonna Breonna Breonna Breonna Breonna Breonna
Breonna Breonna Breonna Breonna Breonna Breonna
Breonna Breonna Breonna Cassius Breonna Breonna
Breonna Breonna Breonna Breonna Breonna Breonna
Breonna Breonna Breonna Breonna Breonna Breonna
Breonna Breonna Breonna Breonna Breonna Breonna
Breonna Breonna Breonna Breonna Breonna Breonna
Breonna Breonna Breonna Breonna Breonna Breonna
Breonna Breonna Breonna Breonna Breonna Breonna
Breonna Breonna Breonna Breonna Breonna Breonna
Breonna Breonna Breonna Breonna Breonna Breonna
Breonna Breonna Breonna Breonna Breonna Breonna
Breonna Breonna Breonna Breonna Breonna Breonna

4

Breonna Breonna Breonna Breonna Breonna Breonna
Breonna Breonna Breonna Breonna Breonna Breonna
Breonna Breonna Breonna Breonna Breonna Breonna
Breonna Breonna Breonna Breonna Breonna Breonna
Breonna Breonna Breonna Breonna Breonna Breonna
Breonna Breonna Breonna Breonna Breonna Breonna
Breonna Breonna Breonna Breonna Breonna Breonna
Breonna Breonna Breonna Breonna Breonna Breonna
Breonna Breonna Breonna Breonna Breonna Breonna
Breonna Breonna Breonna Breonna Breonna Breonna
Breonna Breonna Breonna Breonna Breonna Breonna

Breonna Breonna Breonna Breonna Breonna Breonna
Breonna Breonna Breonna Breonna Breonna Breonna
Breonna Breonna Breonna Breonna Breonna Breonna
Breonna Breonna Breonna Breonna Breonna Breonna
Breonna Breonna Breonna Breonna Breonna Breonna
Breonna Breonna Breonna Breonna Breonna Breonna
Breonna Breonna Breonna Breonna Breonna Breonna
Breonna Breonna Breonna Breonna Breonna Breonna
Breonna Breonna Breonna Breonna Breonna Breonna
Breonna Breonna Breonna Breonna Breonna Breonna
Breonna Breonna Breonna Breonna Breonna Breonna
Breonna Breonna Breonna Breonna Breonna Breonna
Breonna Breonna Breonna Breonna Breonna Breonna
Breonna Breonna Breonna Breonna Breonna Breonna
Breonna Breonna Breonna Breonna Breonna Breonna
Breonna Breonna Breonna Breonna Breonna Breonna
Breonna Breonna Breonna Breonna Breonna Breonna
Breonna Breonna Breonna Breonna Breonna Breonna
Breonna Breonna Breonna Breonna Breonna Breonna
Breonna Breonna Breonna Breonna Breonna Breonna
Breonna Breonna Breonna Breonna Breonna Breonna

Breonna Breonna Breonna Breonna Breonna Breonna
Breonna Breonna Breonna Breonna Breonna Breonna
Breonna Breonna Breonna Breonna Breonna Breonna
Breonna Breonna Breonna Breonna Breonna Breonna
Breonna Breonna Breonna Breonna Breonna Breonna
Breonna Breonna Breonna Breonna Breonna Breonna
Breonna Breonna Breonna Breonna Breonna Breonna
Breonna Breonna Breonna Breonna Breonna Breonna
Breonna Breonna Breonna Breonna Breonna Breonna
Breonna Breonna Breonna Breonna Breonna Breonna
Breonna Breonna Breonna Breonna Breonna Breonna
Breonna Breonna Breonna Breonna Breonna Breonna
Breonna Breonna Breonna Breonna Breonna Breonna
Breonna Breonna Breonna Breonna Breonna Breonna
Breonna Breonna Breonna Breonna Breonna Breonna
Breonna Breonna Breonna Breonna Breonna Breonna
Breonna Breonna Breonna Breonna Breonna Breonna
Breonna Breonna Breonna Breonna Breonna Breonna
Breonna Breonna Breonna Breonna Breonna Breonna
Breonna Breonna Breonna Breonna Breonna Breonna
Breonna Breonna Breonna Breonna Breonna Breonna
Breonna Breonna Breonna Breonna Breonna Breonna
Breonna Breonna Breonna Breonna Breonna Breonna
Breonna Breonna Breonna Breonna Breonna Breonna
Breonna Breonna Breonna Breonna Breonna Breonna
Breonna Breonna Breonna Breonna Breonna Breonna
Breonna Breonna Breonna Breonna Breonna Breonna
Catherine Breonna Breonna Breonna Breonna Breonna
Breonna Breonna Breonna Breonna Breonna Breonna
Breonna Breonna Breonna Breonna Breonna Breonna
Breonna Breonna Breonna Breonna Breonna Breonna

Breonna Breonna Breonna Breonna Breonna Breonna
Breonna Breonna Breonna Breonna Breonna Breonna
Breonna Breonna Breonna Breonna Breonna Breonna
Breonna Breonna Breonna Breonna Breonna Breonna
Breonna Breonna Breonna Breonna Breonna Breonna
Breonna Breonna Breonna Breonna Breonna Breonna
Breonna Breonna Breonna Breonna Breonna Breonna
Breonna Breonna Breonna Breonna Breonna Breonna
Breonna Breonna Breonna Breonna Breonna Breonna
Breonna Breonna Breonna Breonna Breonna Breonna
Breonna Breonna Breonna Breonna Breonna Breonna
Breonna Breonna Breonna Breonna Breonna Breonna
Breonna Breonna Breonna Breonna Breonna Breonna
Breonna Breonna Breonna Breonna Breonna Breonna
Breonna Breonna Breonna Breonna Breonna Breonna
Breonna Breonna Breonna Breonna Breonna Breonna
Breonna Breonna Breonna Breonna Breonna Breonna
Breonna Breonna Breonna Breonna Breonna Breonna
Breonna Breonna Breonna Breonna Breonna Breonna
Breonna Breonna Breonna Breonna Breonna Breonna
Breonna Breonna Breonna Breonna Breonna Breonna
Breonna Breonna Breonna Breonna Breonna Breonna
Breonna Breonna Breonna Breonna Breonna Breonna
Breonna Breonna Breonna Breonna Breonna Breonna
Breonna Breonna Breonna Breonna Breonna Breonna
Breonna Breonna Breonna Breonna Breonna Breonna
Breonna Breonna Breonna Breonna Breonna Breonna
Breonna Breonna Breonna Breonna Breonna Breonna
Breonna Breonna Breonna Breonna Breonna Breonna
Breonna Breonna Breonna Breonna Breonna Breonna

**Breonna Breonna Breonna Breonna Breonna Breonna
Breonna Breonna Breonna Breonna Breonna Breonna**

I am a liar, I am a pig and I will clean up after myself.

**Breonna Breonna Breonna Breonna Breonna Breonna
Breonna Breonna Breonna Breonna Breonna Breonna
Breonna Breonna Breonna Breonna Breonna Breonna
Breonna Breonna Breonna Breonna Breonna Breonna
Breonna Breonna Breonna Breonna Breonna Breonna
Breonna Breonna Breonna Breonna Breonna Breonna
Breonna Breonna Breonna Breonna Breonna Breonna
Breonna Breonna Breonna Breonna Breonna Breonna
Breonna Breonna Breonna Breonna Breonna Breonna
Breonna Breonna Breonna Breonna Breonna Breonna
Breonna Breonna Breonna Breonna Breonna Breonna
Breonna Breonna Breonna Breonna Breonna Breonna
Breonna Breonna Breonna Breonna Breonna Breonna
Breonna Breonna Breonna Breonna Breonna Breonna
Breonna Breonna Breonna Breonna Breonna Breonna
Breonna Breonna Breonna Breonna Breonna Breonna
Breonna Breonna Breonna Breonna Breonna Breonna
Breonna Breonna Breonna Breonna Breonna Breonna
Breonna Breonna Breonna Breonna Breonna Breonna
Breonna Breonna Breonna Breonna Breonna Breonna
Breonna Breonna Breonna Breonna Breonna Breonna
Breonna Breonna Breonna Breonna Breonna Breonna
Breonna Breonna Breonna Breonna Breonna Breonna
Catherine Breonna Breonna Breonna Breonna Breonna
Breonna Breonna Breonna Breonna Breonna Breonna
Breonna Breonna Breonna Breonna Breonna Breonna
Breonna Breonna Breonna Breonna Breonna Breonna**

Breonna Breonna Breonna Breonna Breonna Breonna
Breonna Breonna Breonna Breonna Breonna Breonna
Breonna Breonna Breonna Breonna Breonna Breonna
Breonna Breonna Breonna Breonna Breonna Breonna
Breonna Breonna Breonna Breonna Breonna Breonna
Breonna Breonna Breonna Breonna Breonna Breonna
Breonna Breonna Breonna Breonna Breonna Breonna
Breonna Breonna Breonna Breonna Breonna Breonna
Breonna Breonna Breonna Breonna Breonna Breonna
Breonna Breonna Breonna Breonna Breonna Breonna
Breonna Breonna Breonna Breonna Breonna Breonna
Breonna Breonna Breonna Breonna Breonna Breonna
Breonna Breonna Breonna Breonna Breonna Breonna
Breonna Breonna Breonna Breonna Breonna Breonna
Breonna Breonna Breonna Breonna Breonna Breonna
Breonna Breonna Breonna Breonna Breonna Breonna
Breonna Breonna Breonna Breonna Breonna Breonna
Breonna Breonna Breonna Breonna Breonna Breonna
Breonna Breonna Breonna Breonna Breonna Breonna
Breonna Breonna Breonna Breonna Breonna Breonna
Breonna Breonna Breonna Breonna Breonna Breonna
Breonna Breonna Breonna Breonna Breonna Breonna
Breonna Breonna Breonna Breonna Breonna Breonna
Breonna Breonna Breonna Breonna Breonna Breonna
Breonna Breonna Breonna Breonna Breonna Breonna
Breonna Breonna Breonna Breonna Breonna Breonna
Breonna Breonna Breonna Breonna Breonna Breonna
Breonna Breonna Breonna Breonna Breonna Breonna
Breonna Breonna Breonna Breonna Breonna Breonna
Breonna Breonna Breonna Breonna Breonna Breonna
Breonna Breonna Breonna Breonna Breonna Breonna
Breonna Breonna Breonna Breonna Breonna Breonna
Breonna Breonna Breonna Breonna Breonna Breonna
Breonna Breonna Breonna Shades Creonna Breonna
Breonna Breonna Breonna Breonna Breonna Breonna
Breonna Breonna Breonna Breonna Breonna Breonna
Breonna Breonna Breonna Breonna Breonna Breonna
Breonna Breonna Breonna Breonna Breonna Breonna
Breonna Breonna Breonna Breonna Breonna Breonna

Breonna Breonna Breonna Breonna Breonna Breonna
Breonna Breonna Breonna Breonna Breonna Breonna
Breonna Breonna Breonna Breonna Breonna Breonna
Breonna Breonna Breonna Breonna Breonna Breonna
Breonna Breonna Breonna Breonna Breonna Breonna
Breonna Breonna Breonna Breonna Breonna Breonna
Breonna Breonna Breonna Breonna Breonna Breonna
Breonna Breonna Breonna Breonna Breonna Breonna
Breonna Breonna Breonna Breonna Breonna Breonna
Breonna Breonna Breonna Breonna Breonna Breonna
Breonna Breonna Breonna Breonna Breonna Breonna
Breonna Breonna Breonna Breonna Breonna Breonna
Breonna Breonna Breonna Breonna Breonna Breonna
Breonna Breonna Breonna Breonna Breonna Breonna
Breonna Breonna Breonna Breonna Breonna Breonna
Breonna Breonna Breonna Breonna Breonna Breonna
Breonna Breonna Breonna Breonna Breonna Breonna
Breonna Breonna Breonna Breonna Breonna Breonna
Breonna Breonna Breonna Breonna Breonna Breonna
Breonna Breonna Breonna Breonna Breonna Breonna
Breonna Breonna Breonna Breonna Breonna Breonna
Breonna Breonna Breonna Breonna Breonna Breonna
Breonna Breonna Breonna Breonna Breonna Breonna
Breonna Breonna Breonna Breonna Breonna Breonna
Breonna Breonna Breonna Breonna Breonna Breonna
Breonna Breonna Breonna Breonna Breonna Breonna
Breonna Breonna Breonna Breonna Breonna Breonna
Breonna Breonna Breonna Breonna Breonna Breonna
Breonna Breonna Breonna Breonna Breonna Breonna
Breonna Breonna Breonna Breonna Breonna Breonna
Breonna Breonna Breonna Breonna Breonna Breonna

**Breonna Breonna Breonna Breonna Breonna Breonna
Breonna Breonna Breonna Breonna Breonna Breonna
Breonna Breonna Breonna Breonna Breonna Breonna
Breonna Breonna Breonna Breonna Breonna Breonna
Breonna Breonna Breonna Breonna Breonna Breonna
Breonna Breonna Breonna Breonna Breonna Breonna
Breonna Breonna Breonna Breonna Breonna Breonna
Breonna Breonna Breonna Breonna Breonna Breonna
Breonna Breonna Breonna Breonna Breonna Breonna
Breonna Breonna Breonna Breonna Breonna Breonna
Breonna Breonna Breonna Breonna Breonna Breonna
Breonna Breonna Breonna Breonna Breonna Breonna
Breonna Breonna Breonna Breonna Breonna Breonna
Breonna Breonna Breonna Breonna Breonna Breonna
Breonna Breonna Breonna Breonna Breonna Breonna
Breonna Breonna Breonna Breonna Breonna Breonna
Breonna Breonna Breonna Breonna Breonna Breonna
Breonna Breonna Breonna Breonna Breonna Breonna
Breonna Breonna Breonna Breonna Breonna Breonna
Breonna Breonna Breonna Breonna Breonna Breonna
Breonna Breonna Breonna Breonna Breonna Breonna
Breonna Breonna Breonna Breonna Breonna Breonna
Breonna Breonna Breonna Breonna Breonna Breonna**

You never knew that your name had so much power? Both you and **George Floyd** sparked one of the country's biggest doses of civil unrest where people are so tired of not being seen, heard or felt as a majority of minorities. I'm so sorry that Louisville just won't admit they fucked up but I don't PRAY. I HOPE someone can clean up that whole entire Judicial System in Louisville and then turn around and fix it everywhere else where the good old boy Network finally dies.

But I pray today that you can see me reaching out for your hand seeking justice the best way I can. The only way I know how. Hit the cancer at its core and change its DNA. Art for art's sake.

I had all these stories in time. I just needed to get them together. It took a friend of mine, who is dying of cancer, to remind me how precious every moment is with how much life matters. Even if you'll never let me be your last lover I hope that you discover more Beauty in life and take bigger plans to fight the good fight.

I **REFUSE** TO LET MY FATHER'S SINS BE THIS SIN THIS SON.

Homey don't Clay dat

**It's a Duty
Not a Choice
Because there's is
no fucking justice
for Breonna. This
is the best this
white girl's (whose
family freed slaves)
daddy tormenting
your mother can
do.**

I would appreciate it if you leave me to live a more private life because I would love to continue to create w/o worrying what other people think of me. I told my baby, "I'm going to strap you on my back and we're going to run through life like hell." He repeated it back to me 3 years later but I only said it once and I meant it. (So far I haven't been able to run just limp). His first word @ 3 months was "allo" because we were always together and I spoke on the phone.

Having SEVERE brain damage, being in public, PERIOD, is sensory overload. I'm pretty shy which is why I'm not a full time porn star. I just want to teach you how to fuck like one. I don't care to be objectified by YOU even though I'm objectifying myself and my husband (he doesn't mind like he did before not him no not anymore). I'll do Instagrams after I hand you a signed copy but please don't disturb me. I'm scared of living as it tiz. Sometimes

I'll even personalize a copy but most of the time a photo, air kisses and quite possibly a hug but don't ever ask to shake my hand. I've got OCD pretty bad and the pandemic didn't help. It just makes me happy I no longer feel like I HAVE TO shake s man that didn't wash his cock off into mine. :X

If you want to change our lives quickly please vote for me. I stand before you, naked, "Catya Clay Streaker '' transparent to the core, 20th generation American asking to take the reins of the "free" world so we can invest in human capital as we head towards a more egalitarian society. You want true swearing social changes in "god (no one took the God from Goddess) we trust, SchoolHouse Rock, If we don't make these changes today then we only have Extinction to look forward to. Tomorrow. Because you're a blip.

I'll never make it through to "the powers that be" so I'm counting on you to help me unlock our nation's mystery. That one bitch wanting redemption for Trump's Campaign and the sway of how social change is guided by a bunch of White, Corporate interests vs my very simple campaign "WE the PEOPLE" (get Beyonce to finish my theme) In Order to form a more perfect union..." I AM YOUR BITCH. You're going to love my" grassroots" power of the pussy family that started the Democratic-pubes party. Help me be the one to make history as someone with "100 hours" vs "100 days" and implement the power of the pussy. 🐱

I believe in the Republic but we are ANYTHING BUT "Democratic." I am not corrupted by political shit so I'm wearing a different man's outfit. Domestic violence thriver; raped; single; widowed mother; **WOKE**: Russian speaking; seeing the world with a "commoner's eyes;" my matriarchal side carrying the stain from cancer spanning Through Time losing my mom @ 25 as cancer ate her alive; A sister that survived leukemia; Grandma to 92. Addicts in the attic; A husband died in my arms (like mom) with his last breath being,"I love you" as the heart attack from addiction took him away on 4/20 of all the days; Homeless; a tube of pus left to rot in my body 7 years; being pieces of the healthcare crisis unfolding slices; A deadbeat dad that threw us away as he divorced her forcing us to live with him while abusing my mother putting her in an early grave; watching my son fight for life in the NICU; publicly educated and made it through Uni; I'll tell you what my plans are to form a more perfect union; make our lives better and to grow our society so we can all live with life in "sobriety."

Remember I'm always OneOpinionatedBitch.Com so don't come at me looking to bend. You came here looking at me to see what you can do while changing inside core of YOU. I wrote most of this when I had a septic tube in me so each day I think more clearly. Remember I'm like a baby at light speed because my thinking was always ahead of me not being able to think out of anyone's box but my own. Please help me make our country a better home.

If we don't change today there's not much hope for our heirs to live enjoying a life we can no longer promise tomorrow. Make companies responsible for their crimes against humanity while causing Society to live out in mediocrity. Choose somebody who can see what uncle Sam claims to be. Let's believe in ourselves being mindful of millennials instead of tearing them down like so many generations that keep hanging around. Put stock in humans looking to even the score. Quit busting our asses paying taxes so rich people are free to fuck up humanity and our own asses. How much of our lives need to be extinct until we understand we're not truly free as we like to think we will always be while our rights and liberties melt away each day in front of me.

Please help me make history by changing society, giving our lives to our dissipating progenies.

Vote for Catherine Clay when I can run on election day. I'll change our lives... come what may. Thank you for loving me.

Love Always and Forever,

Catherine Elizabeth Clay

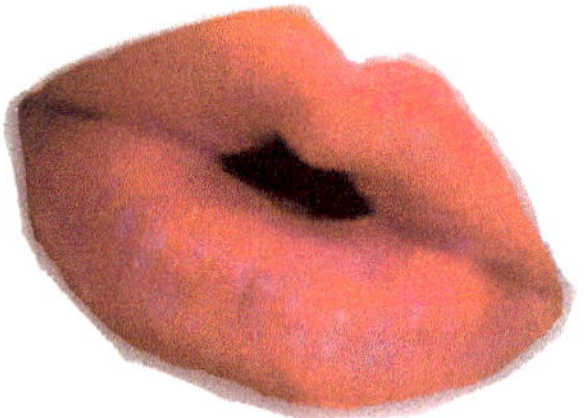

DEARLY BELOVED

I'm celebrating the life I shared with my husband and the deepest, saddest, darkest holes in my heart… an 8th sea of tears to leave behind me and it's only been 5 years of this **Unbearable Lightness of Being**. One of the most horrifying, traumatic days losave the day I came out of my post septic sentence.

5 years of widow cunt, one Tinder fuck, I was the first person that tried online dating in 1996 with Schwalm in Frankfurt when the axe murderers were yet to come into being. (please… if you take me just kill me. I won't be faking orgasms because like a man I CAN'T. I've trained my cunt to gush and she's not happy. I only recently found a lover that has lasted longer than 7 fucks and years of bullshit romance. It's nice. This photo popped up our second time and he got "spooked". "No… He's just happy I'm happy and is just letting us know it's all good."

I repeat myself many times over. Hopefully your neuroptypical mind can handle it. It's hard for me to keep going back trying to make sense of this all.

I loved my husband more than anybody… until Cassius. More than life, literally. It's just a cruel twist of fate that he passed away before me which was so unfair. The shock that happened to me the day before left betrayal after betrayal. Shockwave after Shockwave. He saved my life so many times, I thought, but he also did things that almost took it. 5x. I guess he developed Munchausen's to get the drugs. Being a sex addict and not accepting that my body needed to rest after surgeries :/// But he knew there were so many beats to a human heart. Through all his faults and vanities I will miss him to the depth of every step.

He was my world, my everything. Without him I wouldn't be writing this all now. The Amazing world of evolving sex seen through this iconic eye. His iconic eyes. He was like the shadow over the moon, eklyptic.org. He died at the answer to everything, 42, if you're a fan of **"Hitchhiker's Guide to the Galaxy."**

It's with him that I find most stories in my mind of being the most compatible lover although…

Kevin… I'm sorry I fucked up Kevvy Joe because you have the perfect pole. But you put that condition upon me and it's not fair to say my cunt belonged to you. Of all the lovers I've ever had you're the only one I'd say, "I wish I married you" to but you wouldn't ask me. I made a photograph of us as a married couple and you laughed.

I loved you and you went up against that son of a bitch (dad) in court and came home that night and told me, "**I don't love you anymore.**" But you couldn't give the cunt up and when we jumped off one another because my cunt did what it did that one time… that's **only** been with **you**.

I tried to make 101 stories but when I started reading about how you unleashed the **Ninja Pussy** inside of me you set me free and it was too much to go back and feel those old things with so much more zeal because of how my erotica started to take off and feeling your full lips running all over my tits became all too consuming. So that's how I still feel and can't stop. My feelings are just like my dad said, a **Gordian knot.**

I meant it when I said, "I love you." I just don't believe in monogamy. My cunt only belongs TO ME.

I have yet to discover anyone that can fit as you have. No one measured up in both body and spirit (and nobody talks as filthy as you did but I really hated it when you used to say, "you're more beautiful with my cock inside of you." 🫣) Hopefully the next sadist will be honest enough to tell me upfront.

I chose the guy that drove an old beat up pick up truck because I saw how my grandfather treated my grandmother and died like a real man, taking out the trash. Fuck the Porsche (like my dad… funny story that) you're buying into a car but it's ok for a woman to buy one since there's no need to prove we don't have penis envy.

I never believed in penis envy because I can have any size I want and it will all depend on different shapes and sizes. I can't manifest anyone that could fit into the image that I am except for him. So I fuck myself these days. I plan on doing a little show known as "**Friday Night Delights**" but not for long.

I was hesitant to be a mother (turning Josh into a mother fucker) until he put his head on my belly assuring me that everything would be alright when I found out I was 4 months pregnant (vs my sister that screamed, "have an abortion." But I promised myself a long time ago if I got pregnant I'd never get rid of it. I hated losing my Jr. But she's a dead tissue, just like all the anti abortion acceptable **HATE SPEECH AGAINST WOMEN** that needs to be recognized as **hate speech** and made illegal. Abortion is here to stay for a very good reason. Some people shouldn't be mothers and others shouldn't be fathers.) It has and has not been the tits but I'm looking at the events of my life with open negative **posalividly**.

As a trained photographer I worked with negative film that always turned positives which is what has colored my life with all kinds of rainbows. "**My wife sees rainbows wherever she goes**" Josh wrote in a Facebook post not one to be very sharing.

I'm psychic and with this hole on my soul, an arachnoid cyst, please anyone that wants to acyst.org me, will ya? I can pick up thoughts through vibrations and frequencies. Josh worked for **"The Frequency"** when we got together. He didn't remember our first kiss but the build up began by giving me a foot massage before Brain Surgery #2 while I was still married. I'm glad he inspired **"My First Kiss"**.

Josh was one of the loves of my life but not my soulmate. I'm a Gemini so I'm my own soul mate. He was my Adonis-like mind which I couldn't read inside knowing what would make him tick. After a fight we'd always kiss and make up in front of our son so he learnt conflict resolution until I popped him raping me because I was too fucked up. On too much fentanyl, and it shows as well as the brain damage you now read. YOU fix the Grammar, the cases. "Art for art's sake is supposed to make YOU *think*" ~Catherine Clay, like someone with brain damage, does understand the flaws.

My Adonis grew one site then turned it into 11 for fucking prick and his architecture is still the root of the site. His coding was pure. I begged him to leave but he couldn't leave his 11 babies he created at the beginning of developing websites in 2004. He just never believed in himself. "If you are irreplaceable you are unpromotable." Josh Harris

Nor did he wish to give up our daily routine of breaking the boredom of life working from home (ROTFLMFAO pre covid post covid what **joke's on us**). We were together, forever and always as light beings. Those strongest memories are where we live when we no longer have a body to give. I'll never not appreciate that fucking prick for letting him work from home (today we take THAT for granted) and I'm sorry for how I've reacted but he still deserved 1/3 of your company or at the very least a healthy scholarship for Cassius because you only paid him $58,000 a year when he should have been making 200k at least. I mean NOW you realize how irreplaceable he is. The worst fights we had was that he would not quit working for you because you are such a cheap bastard and you never paid him for his last $6,000 rebuild on plsn and 4k for another but he died before he could ask even though I begged him even the day he died to send you an e-mail you fat, cheap POS.

Josh worked with me for my foundation by being a supporting caregiver and being our webmaster. He was with me in 2004 and was a founder of the **Arachnoid Cyst Foundation** as well as a caregiver. But 3 days before he died he started looking into creating apps but they were dreams that didn't come to fruition. He just never believed in himself.

His knowledge of the internet was as vast as all his appetites that reeked of sensual pleasures. All five senses worked in delight with Shakespearian proportions making him burn so bright in so many people's light. When he died it was a horrific plight for so many to show so much love but their love did not mirror his. I always told him he was oblivious; he just chose to show you all just what love truly is vs. you listening to him and being sensitive to HIS feelings. I did the best I could by being dissed for all of my abilities. All I have to say is fuck all your "friends" that never gave you a shoulder to cry up on because Burbank High '92 you stood on top of his shoulders shocked to death to knew what he could do.

Fucking sportsmanship reality of women's mentality has to be rearranged because soccer is a sport but date rape is just cruel and too many of you little fucks have that mentality. Unless I am shown respect as one of the world's greatest lovers of life we'll never see eye to eye because that's what he should inspire in us as our muse. Time won't heal this wound from what I've discovered but I've learnt how to always recover and hope the next one will forever remain as someone with whom I want to play.

I have to start generating an income so that's why I will be selling my soul as I knew this day would cum. Dreamt the day would come when I could be my most inventive putting everything together. My manifest destiny My ongoing legacy. My art for art's sake.

When I saw the size of his balls I went "Mama." He'd been pleasing me all night, got up to leave, put his pants on over a painful hard on after eating and playing with my **Ninja Pussy** and I asked him, **"where are you going?"** We had such a good time and I discovered that night that this **Greedy**, hungry **Ninja pussy** could finally be satiated for the entire weekend. He had no refractory period (I have found this to be the case with all but 2 men I've been with since and they were 2 old). We didn't leave bed that first weekend. But I'm giving too much away for "**My First Kiss.**"

Once we started our relationship I quit writing and dedicated my life to enriching all of our lives with the time that we have. We'd all do art in art books and save them so we have a vast collection of all the details of what makes life worth living for our descendants. His thoughts were pure, kind and he was unconditionally loving of all that was me as well as everybody. Unconditional to everybody and all living things he held an awe and respect for them all. Even barefoot slipping in shit at **Woodstock '94**.

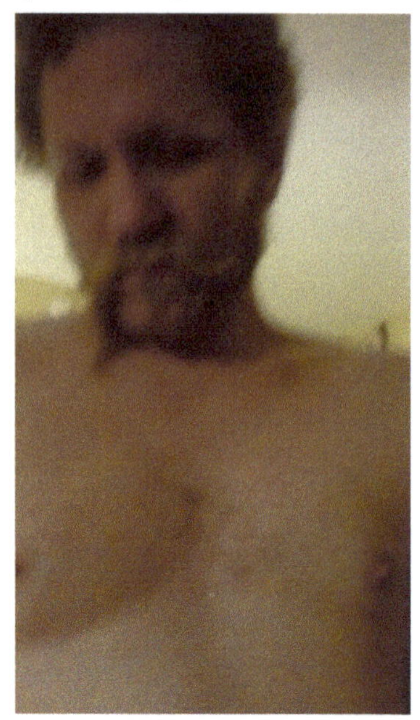

But we were also in an open relationship. Only I was more open with my legs (with lovers I'd already had been with before Josh) and he with his time.

After what my father put me through there was no WAY I was not going to share his big, beautiful cock to anyone that wanted to rock. I had trained him and he would talk about his fantasies that tragically never came to realities. When we got married I knew that sometime down the road it might happen but as long as he came home to mama it was all just gravy for me except for our last anniversary.

I do have a plaster cast of Josh's cock which was **hard** to make (Groucho Eyebrows) . I'm looking into developing vibrators so you will all be able to fuck yourself with **Josh** while drinking your **Josh** whine too.

My mom said that most men would just be happy with a blow job but I found that not to be true. It's just a nice addition to be doing what you do. My husband knew ``**If You Start Me Up...**" A quickie for us was 45 minutes.

As I'm finishing my book, I am much more at ease because I have to admit I am pleased, **blowing fingers rubbing on breasts** and looking forward to the new prey for this Clay. So many memories sizzle my mind and I know when our energy converged we made energy that blew everything through it. The **tymey whimey thing that wibbles and wobbles** (David Tenent please... can we have tea?) I wanted to be the first woman **Dr. Who**. Maybe the first American :O

I love my little guy. Our mini me, my sea of tranquility and the source of all my inspiration as a libation. He's the one that brought the lighting to my pituitary gland making me realize how deep pleasure comes from that spark of life most will never find deep **Inside Yourself**. Things that you cannot feel because the things in your brain aren't physically real like the one over my pituitary gland that makes me sense all the different pieces of essence.

My parents and his parents were eternally loving to each other when they loved each other or they wouldn't have made two lovers so perfectly fit for each other.

"Till death" did we part I'll love you forever and always.

The last thing he said to me was, "**I love you**."

I'm over being hurt and angry because you drove me crazy but just as YOU, **DEAR READER** I let you go to live eternally into the hearts and minds of all that makes this life divine, my darling Valentines.

I'm so sorry YOU NEED THERAPY for all my **PTSDs** that fuck you up so graciously. If you are finding it difficult for you then you need help not me making your life's struggles look like a Goddamn joke. I cannot help you get through my PTSD because you can't function in your own goddamn neurotypical reality made up by our "society." Perhaps you should get off your ass and go live a little bit of life before you condemn mine.

The last bitch that told me I needed therapy I laughed at her because she couldn't deal with MY reality. And this was before I found out I had a surgical leftover tube in my gut filled with septic

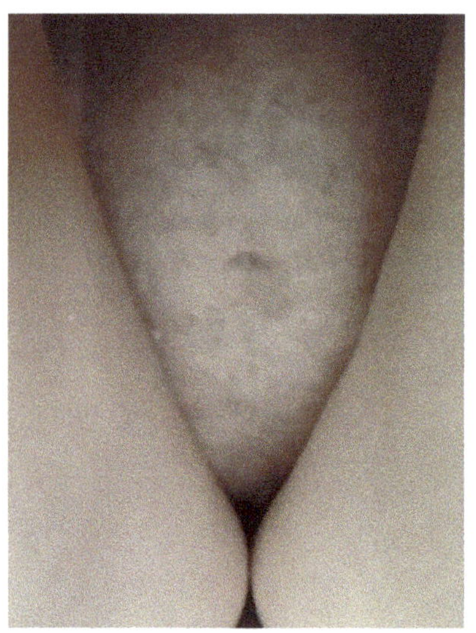

rot and pus for 7 years on Oct 6th. Needless to say I wasn't making the best decisions for anybody in my life and lost too many friends from all my strife.

I wish there was more acceptance of those people fighting your disabilities. It's a tragedy that you lose all sense of reality when your life gets fucked. We just have to remember with every negative there is always a positive result which is how I have to look at life being an old school photographer.

My life is a well written 20 generations of American history with a metric fuck ton of tragedy but I take it in stride because I have to be smiling through the tears of joy making me any my son happy boys one on one.

I miss you, baby.

IN THE BEGINNING...

I'm making you see all men are created equal. Some of you are but the rest of us are superhuman.

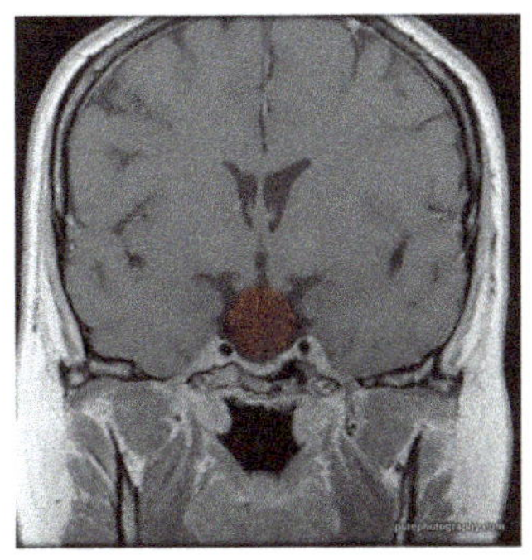

I'm tired y'all. Not just tired, exhausted. I had surgery on October 10th, and living my new life is taking a little getting used to. There's a new world order and I'm not going back and rereading the things I just wrote about myself. I'm sorry I have to try and work through a different story and I'm going to be finished with this book so I can work on my next one. So you get to read a few things over and over and remember... If you need help reading things about my life don't call the suicide hotline cuz they just tell you to call a friend. Get a licensed, trained **EMDR** professional to help you make it through the day trying to figure out how you could navigate my life.

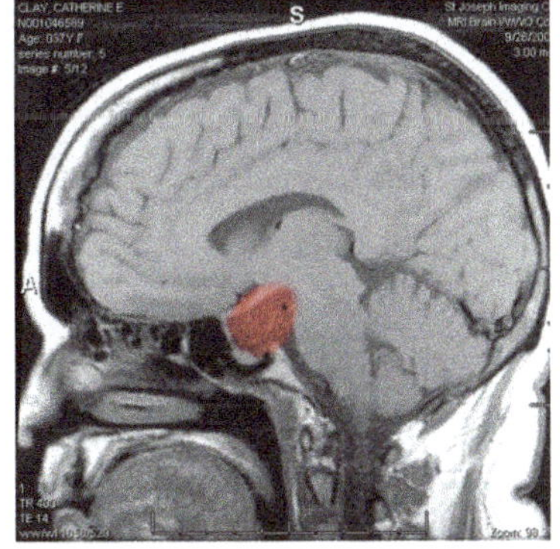

Because I would really like to have somebody who's been through more shit and knows more stuff than me tell me how I need to live my life, mentor or see life the way that I guide you to live yours. No matter what I've been through I always try to keep a smile on my face.

I see which new disease I can conquer this year (I already have carpal tunnel in my right hand CHOSEN for '22 but the mystery guest is always fun!) So I'm sorry you have to read these things a few times but I think your fragile little ego can handle it. If mine can yours can too and remember you're a goddamn neurotypical and look what I've done with my life.

You called us disabled? You couldn't live in my brain DAMAGED (injuries you get to heal from while **DAMAGE** is a **LIFE Sentence, the gift that always {or never} quits giving**) world. I can barely live in my world. I still can't believe I had a fucking tube stuck in my belly w/septic pus for 7 years.

If I could write this feeling as shitty as I did back when I started to write this then you have absolutely **NO EXCUSE** as to why you're not getting your shit done. Quit procrastinating and putting your ideas to somebody else's life. Try not paying attention to other people and see how much further in life you get especially if you don't have to depend on anybody. Depending on someone is the worst thing you can do if you need to be free to let your mind see. That's a cage you can never rearrange and I'm about to be dancing on a volcano.

You know it's those people that you never think about that start something? It wasn't like MLK *poof* "I have a dream" then *poof* He woke up. He had a tremendous amount of support and tragically didn't get to see the results his positive influence had upon the world.

I, on the other hand, have. I've followed your dream and one upped you. Because in this life that's all you can do is follow a dream to help make it come true. Like throwing a penny in a well maybe we can stop us all from going to hell.

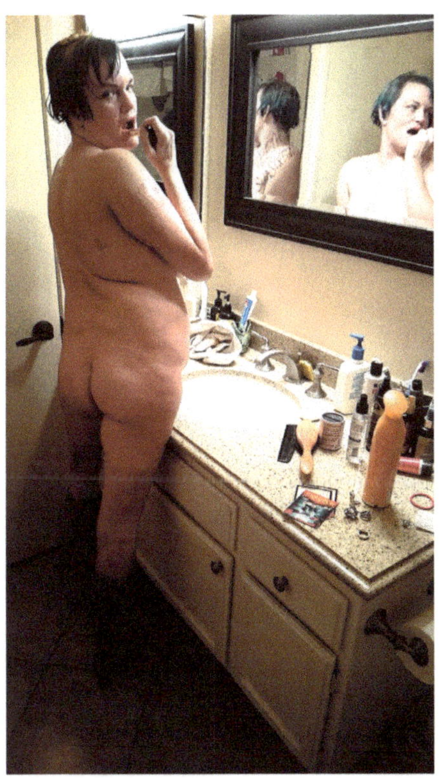

Much like my **Wishing Upon a Star** to live with my mother my son always wished for his mother to get better which I have in spades. But first I got much much worse. So bad I couldn't even tell.

I have had a lot of support utilizing my techniques on how to get a girl to ejaculate. I am that one person that wrote the 1st article on **"The Gentle Art of Female Ejaculation AKA How to Fuck Like a Porn Star."**

THE GENTLE ART OF FEMALE EJACULATION AKA HOW TO FUCK LIKE A PORN STAR.

If it weren't for Andy D. I'd never have known what I do today. My first love until death. But you have to remember that was 20 years ago and I've only gotten better, baby!

I do not encourage people to have sex when they're teenagers. Too many problems and not enough solutions, getting hurt as a teenager vs. being hurt as an adult with a lot different results. I waited until I was twenty before I had sex. Seeing a girl's back seat after bleeding like a stuck pig didn't hurt as well as my parent's first abortion when my mother was 16. She told me in graphic detail about the abortion and how she stuck a coal hanger up her cunt to kill... herself.

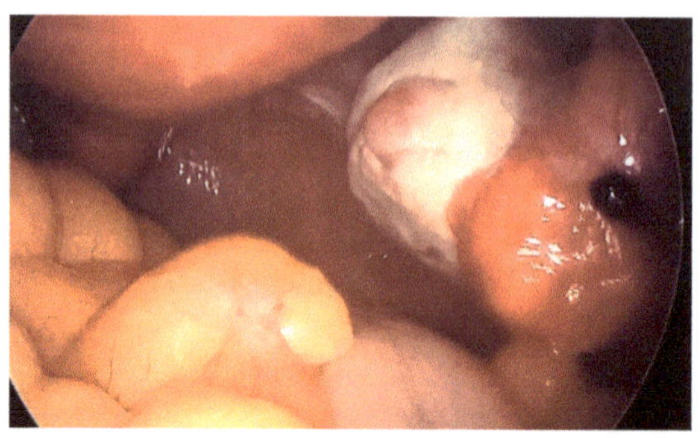

THIS IS WHY FEDERAL GOVERNMENT NEEDS TO TAKE EACH STATE'S ASSUMPTIONS OVER OUR WOMBS AWAY AND MAKE ANTI-ABORTION SPEECH IN LEGISLATION A HATE CRIME AGAINST WOMEN.

Because that's exactly what they are. **HATE CRIMES.** "I hate you for giving me the opportunity to **choose** if I wanted to FORCE that God damn apple shoved down my throat. Bullshit like, "bleeding was a woman's shame" for being kicked out of **The Garden of Earthly Delights. Ya can't trust something that plays for 7 days and doesn't die.** 👆 Who the fuck cares whatever goddamn religion it is it's fucked up. (And you stupid cunts that give these dicks money to "support the community" try and ask them for any money when you don't really need it and see if you get 1 red ¢. They're playing pocket pull with your money! My money manager said he hates these **GUYS** the most. If they need money, let's see how much is on the plate and how it's spent.)

A 13 year old girl raped by her grandfather does not need permission from the state to get an abortion no matter how late the gestation may be... even if she's dilated ready to have it. It's only a human once it breathes! The state sure as fuck isn't going to take care of it. We don't want a welfare system but were living in a welfare state and until many politicians are run the fuck out of office (like every God damn mother fucker that thinks it's a good idea for **Monsanto to NOT** have to account for their **crimes against humanity** including KNOWING they are causing cancer and making that a **law that Americans can't sue them**. 👆 FUCK YOU 👆 "**WE the PEOPLE**" NOT "Corporations for the people that come after the bottom line." We will be able to DNA the cancer and its source of cause for centuries to come because the solutions people who don't live a life they make judgments for humanity.

I started this book when I read **50 Shades** (a story enacted by James Spader and Maggie Gyllenhaal in the movie **The Secretary**) and laughed when she didn't want to be fisted. She shore as fuck didn't know what she was missing. Girls don't only scissor cut... and a girl has a bigger arm. The author's depth of characters... moving. Made me cum... as if. So I said, "write what you know."

I started writing well over 20 years ago when I started keeping the world's oldest online journal, **DearDementedDiary.Com**. (back then monitors only had 101 Shades of Gray)

I have a brain tumor you get the age with so I knew there was ***no doubt*** about the dementia only I

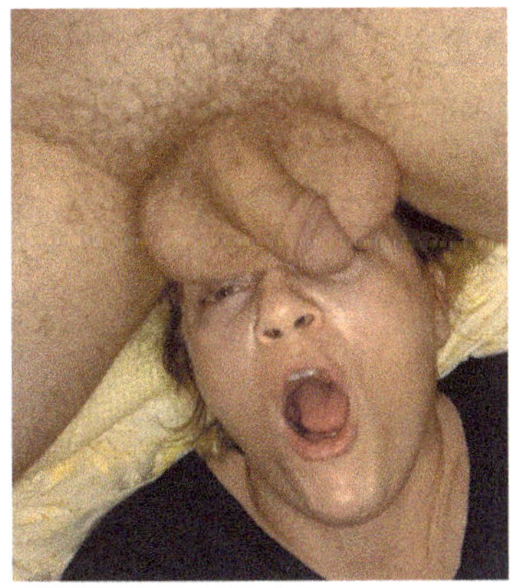

didn't realize just how demented so many situations I've been in turned out.

The boy that sparked my lust is one of the reasons I finished putting this book together. Thank you Gregg... for the most part, because it took him 2 years to tell me he was dying and I didn't want to waste any time getting him to realize that I am worthy and not a waste of sperm. I fell in lust with him 33 years ago and that, my gentle readers, is a lifetime. But he's just going to blow me.

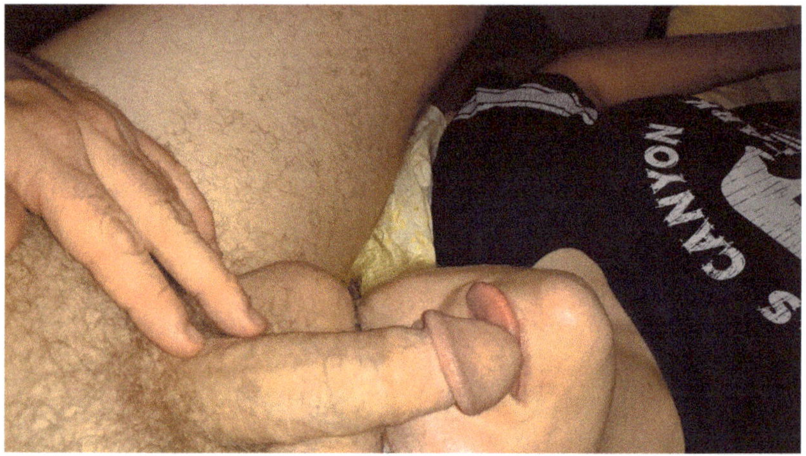

There are several points I want to make in this book besides learning how to use your cunt. It's about health and understanding. If you think this bitch is going to give you some kind of validation for being a Holy Roller go fuck yourself. I'm a better Christian than you. I'll prove it. Let me show you my cunt that's how transparent I am. Let me tell you about being a profit.

One main reason for writing this is to emphatically declare that you need to learn about your own body and how it works. You can say you have a vagina and guess what? That's ONLY a vagina because then you have labia, INNER LABIA (apply suction here), clit, cervix, etc. so let's just call a ♠ a ♠ and a cunt a cunt. Look up the etymology yourself. It is indeed enlightening. (I didn't name DDD Vol II "Tales of the Uncontrollable Cunt" without humor.)

My cunt has all the intricate pieces that come together to make her... reve like a V16.

But enough about my cunt NOW BEING A CUNT and being able to scream out loud and proud is another different story because I'm about to do some very cunty things.

All I wanted was love. Love, affection and the attention my father could never even give me that little. I've scraped and tried to muster some kind of love but when somebody tells you they don't love you because, "you look like" the other parent there's not a lot you can do about that except try and move on. And with my brain damage, psychotic episodes where I was being overdosed with fentanyl and put on other MS drugs that didn't work I kept hoping to get my father's attention the only way I was taught. If you said being a cunt you're **RIGHT**! He tried to sick the FBI on me after all of this stuff I've been through I started to think recently... wait a second a ♠'s a ♠, right?

My daddy issues are big. Not just big but **ASTRONOMICAL**. By the time you get to the end of this book you will understand everything that's why I can give over 101 reasons to say " 👆 fuck you 👆 old man. You're going to *WISH* you'd died of Covid you heartless fuck. Or I had died when I tried really hard @19 or giving birth to **YOUR DYNASTY.** All these fucking accolades and Mercedes collection in "**A Day in the Life of** a racist, heartless cocksucker named **Thomas E Clay**" on my and mother's birthdays in 2021. But not 1 fucking 'world's best grandpa' from the only son that passed on "the family name." 👆

But as we all know wishes are horses (I have no desire to clean up a bunch of horse chit) and I never had a horse. My SISTER had a horse. I never wanted one. I didn't ask for one. When I received sugarcubes I gave up ever having a Merry Christmas knowing my father, "**Mean 'Ol Mr Tooth Decay**" was Santa. Anne saw her horse twice.

Now as most experts would tell you promiscuity is a sign of sexual abuse. Just like happy families being alike we were **"unhappy in its own way."~Tolstoy** and our father CHOSE to keep us very, very UNHAPPY. For HIS financial gain because he never really saw US, "the **girls**" as a package deal because he only wanted my JR. Dynasty I'm telling you.

"The girls" didn't exist when Tomass' played racquetball, chess, went to boy movies (but introduced us to S&M with 9 to 5; we HAD to watch him lose soccer games, we had to watch him get the Atari ; when our dad finally got us a great gift (a huge TV) it was for him! because he came and took it out of our room later; Jr cheated his way through a 20k high school, St Francis, while "public school" was "good enough" for us. I loved telling daddy mom finished his last class but hey... like father, like son! So yes, I was sexually abused this way among more explicit means to decimate any kind of humanity I imbibe.

Now I'm sorry I'm happy I was born a woman because I don't have **penis envy**. I'm never going to look at another black man and wonder, "I wonder if he really has a BBC?" Because there's one thing I've learned about black men, not one.... Not one fucking black man has a little cock like a white boy. White boys have to prove their worth by making money. Black men just need to stay away from cops. And racist attorneys like YOU.

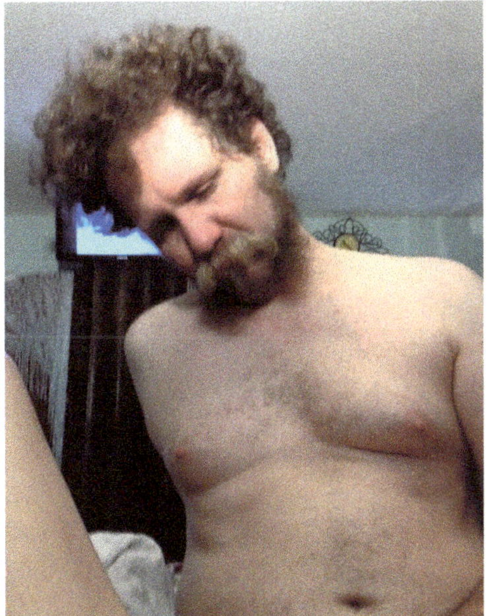

Because of the feminism in the 80s, the post-feminist were able to emerge from diatribe of women that had written their paths in life by following the paths men set for them. Burning their bras before they realize they needed them.

I'm not her. I'm happy to be multi multi multi multi multi-orgasmic. And I'm talking about **20 different types** of interchangeable orgasms. I think the most I've fucked all at once is 15. But don't quote me on that. No less than 13.

I think it's so awesome that gender neutrality is going on. I never ever thought that we would get to this level of understanding so quickly, considering where we were 20 years ago. It's taken centuries. To accept a gay man, a lesbian fuck... anyone who is different. And good God (don't ever quote the big invisible cock to me because I'm sick of **HIM** At least if he were black he'd be obvious) don't those female impersonators make me feel ugly. I have wanted to ifuck one of them with all their makeup on. I've looked at them and wondered how in the hell they could do all the things that they do because I can barely put on fingernail polish. I'm not the type of Tomboy to go to the salon since I can bend my toes to my face. That's how limber I am at 50 due to **EDS**.

EDS. Ehlers Danlos Syndrome is why I can do these things and why I don't look 50. I have a brain tumor you get to age with, an **Arachnoid Cyst** (a pocket of pus rotting inside your head that "doesn't cause long-term central nervous system disease damage... let's just wait and see how bad you get a disability" and I'm popping a new cyst near my cerebellum). Not enough research done on these because it's not like you should be helping people

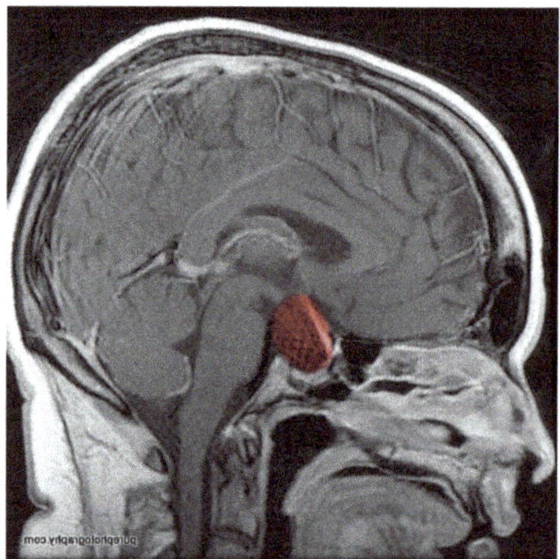

that are going to live with "benign" (w/cancerous results) brain tumors, you should just be helping people that are going to die with them because if that's where the money is.

I'll leave this with you to let **that fact** really sink into your **neurotypical** mindfully mindset.

I've talked a thousands of people and I kind of know what the fuck is going on surviving with an **Arachnoid Cyst.** Our symptoms mimic MS and after a few hateful minutes that's exactly what it starts to blossom into. White mater disease.

Syringomyelia... I think it's my favorite by the way it sounds when it rolls off your tongue. It's a cyst inside your spinal cord that hollows it out with each heartbeat. These have been some fun years, let me tell you. When one doctor sees it and then the rest of them don't but you know… symptoms never lie people just try to fit them into a narrative that makes sense to them. Or their esteemed education.

I walked into Dr William Caton's office when I was 33 and told him I had **syringomyelia** because there are characteristics of it that are specifically tailored to this disease as well as **EDS** and add an **Arachnoid Cyst w/Pseudotumor Cerebri!!!** (kiss fingers blow) The Perfect Storm for a child to suffer long-term ramifications of idiots willing to bring a child with a brain tumor into this world so that it can suffer long term.

Your vanity is not worth your children's sanity. I've only tried to kill myself 4x. All of us try to find relief from faceless suicidal ideations and most of us can't sleep. Yours Truly because mine's in between my optic nerves. When you think about it your eyeballs are always moving so you can't truly rest because you can always feel the cyst pulling on delicate pia mater. Idiots that say, "you can't feel your brain" are just another goddamn neurotypical that will never understand WTF is going on with people that are sick in the head.

Now this is another thing that always makes me scratch my head. Why in the hell do they say that you can't feel things in your brain when the root of your nervous system is the Pia Mater. It's adhered to your arachnoid membrane. The arachnoid membrane serves as the tendrils coming from the roots of your nervous system branch out into the rest of your body.

Since there's a big cyst blocking CSF's way from flowing then brains need rearranging. And those are pieces of bring you might need one day. Or results that ensue make mortality a delicacy not worth savoring every last bit.

Anyway in 2004 Dr Caton ran the MRIs, handed me the reports and walked out of the room saying, "you can read them… Dr Clay" (patients that are chronically ill always know more than their doctors most of the time. Tragically, after 17 years I lost Dr Richard Shubin before the 4th of July. He's the reason I'm still standing). The only thing I didn't recognize was white mater disease on my MRI (enter Dr. Shubin). They can diagnose MS in teenagers now.

With Syringomyelia your vertebrae start to pop open and there aren't enough radiologists that know ANYTHING. Sometimes I can look at my MRI and read it better than one of them, especially the morons that go to Yale.

Now, at 50, I'm popping a new arachnoid cyst in the back of my head instead of just having the one in my spine and in the center of my head.

Now it's the one that's in the center of the head that makes all the difference in the world. Some people, **LIKE ME,** will call you a **child abuser** just like if you cut the tip of your son's cock off. That's called **child abuse.**

The only people that need to have any piece of skin removed from their genitalia are girls so that you can actually see their clitorises and they can come off your body. When a guy gets his teeth stuck in the right position I just go insane. So yes I want to be circumcised just not with a Coke can like they do in Africa. As a child and sew you back up so that you have less than a pinky able for piss and blood to come out of your cunt. And I can't

imagine how blood clots get through those holes. These are the kinds of circumcisions I think we could stay away from.

If somebody wants to mutilate their own bodies that's their business but it's not your business to make a boy's cock smaller than it would be if you had just left it alone.

Do you know where this incessant need to mutilate children comes from? When Nazis pulled down a boy's pants it was kind of easy to tell who was Jewish... so they got so excited to come to America and start circumcising American children so that if there was WWIII Jews would not be cornered because you wouldn't be able to tell who was and who wasn't.

All the hateful propaganda against the poor foreskin and what did it ever do to anybody? Get caught up in some secret spots that women don't know exist because they have never tried one?

God damn I wonder how in the world we had centuries of men with uncircumcised cock living without cancer and other diseases these formidable foreskins hold for the future of mankind. Heidi Fleiss' father was a pediatrician and he regretted every fucking circumcision he ever did.

QUIT ABUSING YOUR CHILDREN. We're the assholes that have to deal with **your** mistakes because **you** can't parent.

Since my cyst is over my pituitary gland it's giving me extra pussy power because I can feel the energy go from my cunt and up to my brain. When Cassius was conceived I know exactly when it happened because lightning went off in my brain. I mean I figured this out later it's not like you have lightning going off on your brain all the time. The only other time I had It go off was when I had an angiogram and that was very painful.

Because my brain is the way it is and because I can feel things that most people can't, I can articulate what it means to have so many vast sensations going off inside of your cunt and mind at the same time. Then identify each little orgasm as it comes and comes and comes again.

I have come so hard I had to ceiling and I don't think any other man on the planet can say that. I know I've come so much that we thought I was going to die because there was so much girl cum everywhere. Imagine **The Texas Chainsaw Massacre** but instead of blood its girl cum. Easily 70% of my water.

And if left laying around long enough you can tell girl cum smells **A LOT DIFFERENT** than piss. So if you can't handle a man cumming **more than you** on top of having 20 orgasms to release the Kraken you better get cracking. I am told there is nothing that feels like a nice hot shot to the balls. The only problem is it starts to get cold. But it's not as much fun having a cold ass smacked by said balls. That's why you need to ejaculate AGAIN. And again. Et. All.

47

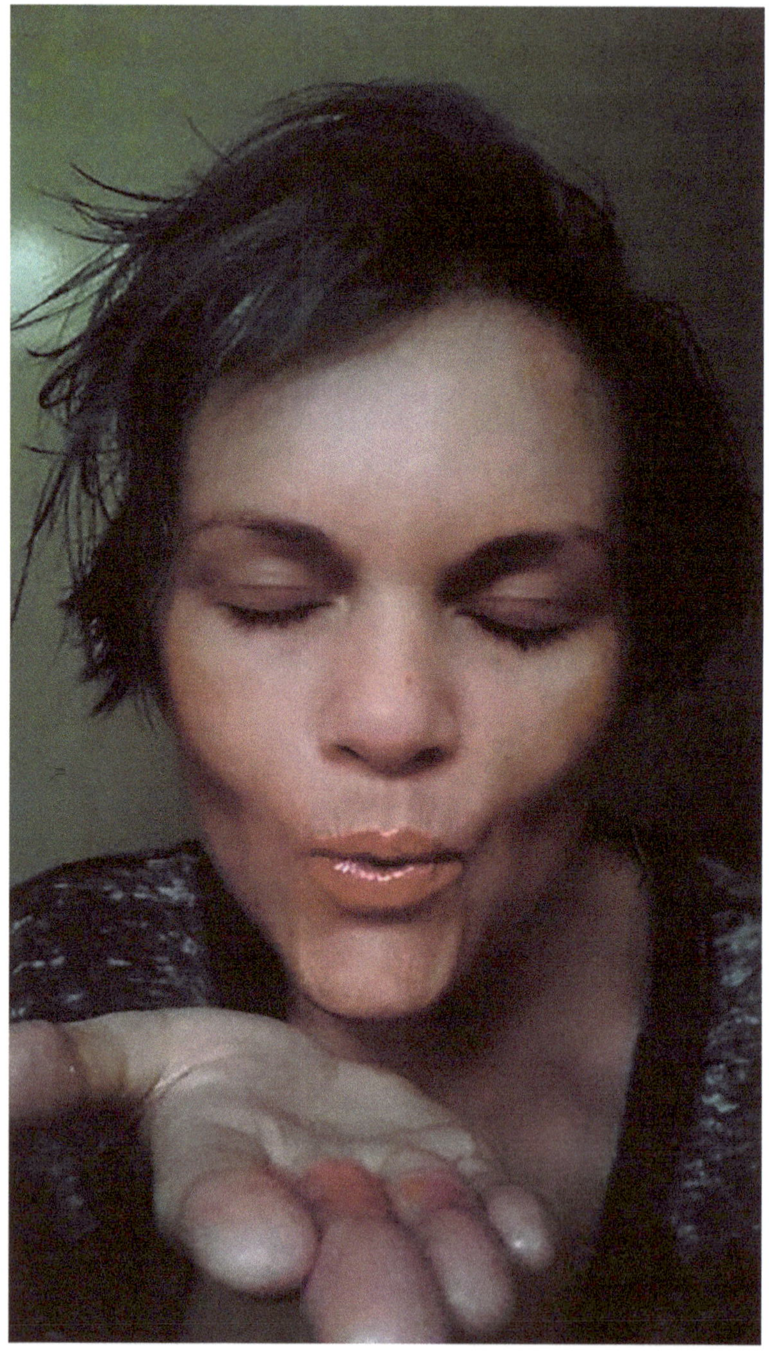

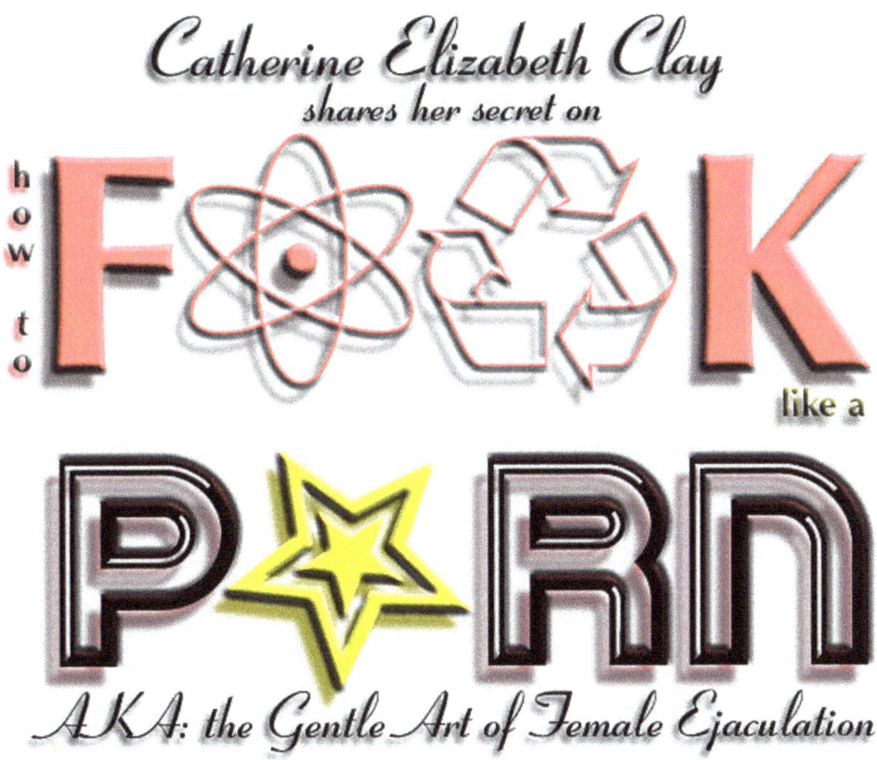
Catherine Elizabeth Clay
shares her secret on
how to
F**K
like a
P★RN
AKA: the Gentle Art of Female Ejaculation

Ladies, you need to learn how to use your body and not be afraid of asking for pleasure from your partner. Or simply learn this all by yourself. Just relax and enjoy their touch. Have a glass of wine, get high or do whatever you can loosen up. Take a hot bath, so all your muscles are relaxed. Make sure you use the bathroom so there is no doubt that you didn't urinate.

The orgasms you experience with FE are different then the clitoral stimulation. They are more all body orgasms that do different things to different people.

To get a feel for where the G-spot is, you are going to have to have her comfortably positioned on her back. Lubrication is essential so try to be passionate and not so technical and make sure you have an abundance of towels ready. Reach up inside of her with your palm facing the ceiling. This is where one embarrassing moment may come for you girls because you are going to have to bear down on him as if you were trying to expel something from your body, and your body will respond in kind... in other words, flatulence is inevitable. My husband used to say, "you're farts smell like roses." Considering the view I must agree. So far AWAY!! (my videos show just a little bit more and make you understand at least how I am multi multi multi multi orgasmic)

So you will have your hand in her and as she bears down on your fingers, or you can feel it by yourself. When you're excited enough you can feel your shaft pop up when you put your hands inside from your clit up into your vag.

You will feel a piece inside her pop out. Chances are she doesn't know it's there because she has never been stimulated in such a manner, and it's not that easy to find on your own. But it's not impossible, just a little difficult. When you feel that part of her pop out, feel it out and just rub your fingertips all over it. Just rub and rub and rub and she will get this overwhelming sensation to pee...

But that's not pee. It doesn't come out like pee, it doesn't smell like pee, and it doesn't taste like pee or have the consistency either. It's thinner and more acidic. If you don't empty your bladder you will pee. It happens to the best of us when you're just too horny to stop. Girl cum is the fluid produced by the skene's gland which will allow you to say, "Baby... I'm going to come in your face."

Allow your body to release that fluid and you have had your first female ejaculatory orgasm. Sometimes you can cum like a trickle, other times you can cum like a fountain, and still others you can cum like ol' fucking faithful, which is why you need the towels. If he starts getting really good you should invest in a waterproof pad so he doesn't get a bunch of girl come all over your bed. There is nothing that smells like days old girl cum.

And it's not like a clitoral orgasm, either. If you are doubling up and stimulating her with your hand and your mouth, then she will have two very different kinds of orgasms. If you get a vaginal orgasm that Trifecta I call "The Grandma." All 3 @ once.

As she is bearing down on you you have to push harder to get in and as you tap the head of your penis on her G-Spot. I call this method **RESISTANCE TRAINING**. Kegels might strengthen your pelvic floor but resistance training makes his cock get bigger because he has to push harder to get inside of you. as well as making your cunt stronger so that it's going to be kind of hard for you to have incontinence as you age. You should have seen the difference between the massive power at the base of my husband's cock was and how much thicker it was after 11 years.

{{When I was younger, 26, I was being hit at the right angle, like holding my hips in a triangle and he penetrated me so deep I squirted so hard I hit the ceiling. I'm the only man that can say that. It's in my book **Dear Demented Diary Volume II Tails of the Uncontrollable Cunt** ;}}

If you add a Vag orgasm because electricity travels up your little tiny suction cups of our vaginas. Like an **Octopus' Garden in the Shade.**

It's kind of hard to get all three at once. But it's easy to knock multiple multiple multiple orgasms once you get some of these techniques down. Once you get your pussy humming.

As she bears down on you and you have to push harder to get in and as you tap the head of your penis on her G-Spot, well, you tell me how it works for you!

When I wrote this article in 1997 I didn't realize that I could still learn different orgasms. I read **The One Hour Butterfly Orgasm** and that is quite an orgasm to have. The unicorn of orgasms.

So there's the **upper G-spot** and a **lower G-spot** and they both give you different types of orgasms because some can give

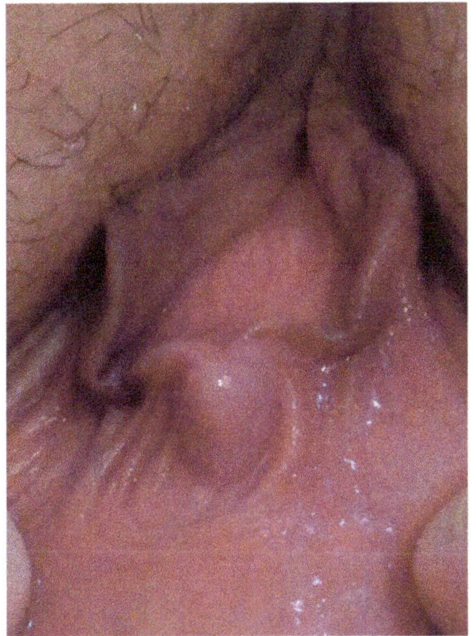

you a trickle and others a squirt on the other **HAND** one's going to give you a nice **gushing orgasm** for your balls to be swinging hot and then cold.

Think of the **G-Spot** like a mushroom with a soft interior on one side and a soft interior on the other side as well as on each side as I found out when I had an **ultrasound orgasm**. Some little cunt told me my anatomy was no different than another woman and she was really quiet after I popped my **G-spot** and wouldn't let it go down. I wish they made vibrators that would do that circle around your G spot.

If your hand is small enough to go up inside of a woman then bonus!!! Because fisting only enhances both the effects of the 2 **G-Spot** orgasms you can have because it stimulates all of those hot pockets. When your **lower G-spot** is hit you still have nerves that tickle your fancy a little bit but the nerves on the **upper G-spot** cause a different orgasm because the sensations are deeper.

As a dude is muff diving I like to feel just a little of teeth peeling back the hood of my clitoris and dragging along my head. We are all girls in the womb, nipples, so a clitoris looks like the head of a penis when you peel back the layers. If anybody needs to be circumcised it's women when they get older because you can remove your clit so that it's exposed more than a little bit. Keep part of your foreskin and get rid of the part keeping your clit attached to your body. But that's something that's an entirely different conversation because I think we all just want the best Sensations and not just with your body but blow your mind in a dumbfounded stupor once you've cum and cum and won't quit pouting.

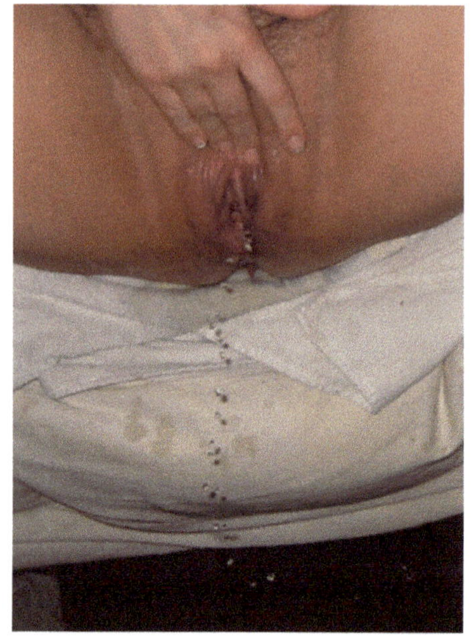

Fisting can cause you to have a **butterfly orgasm** (your uterus drops down when you have a baby so that's what a **Venus butterfly orgasm** is) if your cock is big enough to fit into the cervix, tapping on the upper and **lower G-spot** and massaging the uterus, or womb... eyes in the back of my head and Toes curled.

That doesn't include clit, vag and anal then you have a whole different ball game altogether singing a symphony of so many different multiple orgasms you can have practicing resistance training on a cock to make it grow stronger and bigger not just from getting a hard-on..

1   Lower G-spot (I just taught)
2. Clit (I just showed you)
3. Vag (self explanatory)
4. All 3 @ once =grandma orgasm
5. Eargasms (obvious the start)
6. Upper G-spot (like the lower with more of a kick)
7. Ultrasound orgasm (I can't wait for the vibrator to hook around your g-spot)
8. Anal (self explanatory)
9. Cervical (the 4th set of lips a woman has with just a few of you able to kiss which makes fisting so pleasurable)
10. Uterine (cramps only the opposite. More intense than scissoring because a woman's arm is larger than a man's penis but dyke jokes just aren't what they used to be growing up, gosh darn it. Because men couldn't FATHOM making a joke about a woman's hand being a *perfect* fit [ladies mine was with an Indian dude. Not that I'm against women it's just after my only experience with one I said, "fuck... bitches be crazy. Men can have THEM ALL. So I'm a 50 year old virgin holding out for Miley or Evan. Evan's closer to my age, not to be agest but damn y'all geezers shouldn't be something to shoot for. +/- 15 years will save you grief in the long run [which is what some of this book is about. Just like scrubbing bubbles I did **"the cleaning so you don't have to"** and I have more in common with Evan because her beauty, like my mom used to tell me, "you're more beautiful on the inside" because you're the youest you can be and I stand next to you. Just be glad you didn't have that thing's child])
11. Ovarian (shuddering your entire girlie system)
12. Grandpa Orgasm more than 7 orgasms
13. Pregnant Orgasms (nothing like have 2 things growing inside of you fighting for the space. Fuck as much as possible. Take

early maternity leave just for the occasion because you'll never look at that other person the same after)

14. Butterfly (When women describe having an orgasm during childbirth is from all the pieces coming down. The book **The One-Hour Orgasm: How to Learn the Amazing "Venus Butterfly" Technique** describes it better than me)

15. Fisting (self explanatory but there are things you need to know first)

16. Great Grandma 11 or more at the same time

17. Gushing Orgasms (comes with upper, cervical, uterine and Venus Butterfly

18. Auto Erotic Affixation (I'm not trying this without a doctor)

19. (how could I possibly forget) Blow Jobs (I can come giving as well as receiving)

20. (and) Double Penetration (I've only done this with toys)

21. Cuntilingus. I saved the best for last

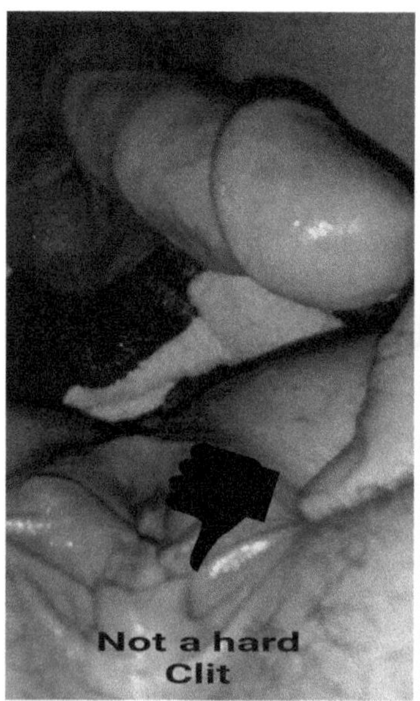

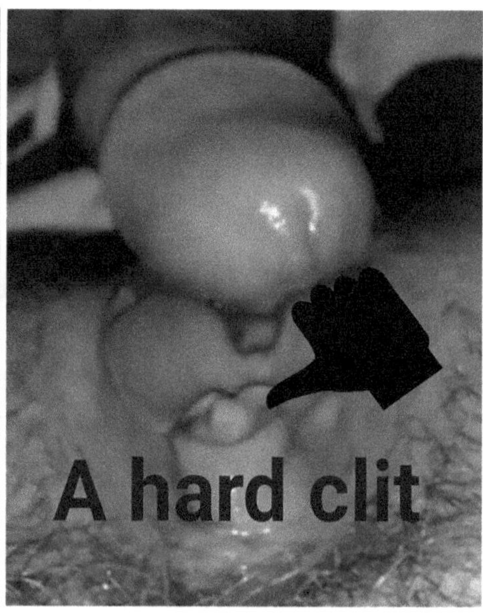

I TOUCH MYSELF

I didn't realize there was anything different from me than another boy until my body betrayed me as I blossomed my heaving bosom. At 8 I was busted in the closet with another boy. I saw his penis the day before but really didn't understand what it was because I didn't understand what I had. But his mother filled me with enough Catholic guilt so I understood that I should never touch my vagina. So I didn't. That was when I was eight. I still, to this day, use a wad of toilet paper to wipe my cunt so I don't have to touch it.

I had this nasty doctor used both fingers then slide the coldest, wettest device inside me making me scream, teaching me this was not a place to touch. It was not sacred. This place never belonged to ME even though it was a part of MY body. It was where I learned that every woman had to take it and every man was the one to give it. The legacy in which my father left me with.

It was the first day of 5th grade and I'd missed it. It was Monday, light years away before I would be in my mother's arms crying about how my father had molested me using a doctor instead of just asking me if I had been molested. She knew what had happened and she would python love all the agony I held inside of me.

It left me feeling trepidation for the entire male population as the minor pleasures would elicit feelings of romantic joy.

A back rub for my father and uncle. The way I kissed one of the boys in the boat house. Feeling my awakening made me feel visceral. That my body was never going to belong to me but rooms inside, pieces of my mind that even I can't see memories too raw I can't reach.

I found myself while listening to Sonic Youth's PCH racing down in the covers wondering. Feeling all I could think of making my own fireworks go off in my head but it was reserved for tantalizing delights I was not ready to share. I was 15 and mentally aware with my own room to finally figure myself out.

The first time I was aware I was different down there was not with the baths that I shared with my brother, even though my mother irritated the story of when I "returned from the hospital someone cut off my tinker," my brother cried his little mind blown that not everybody had a penis large enough to show. They gave me a gift.. The gift of being female.

Nor was it the time my neighbor, in my discoveries where my neighbor would pull his pants down, in the sand yard as my panties were moved to the side.

My favorite joke always goes with this little cocksucker pulling his pants down and screaming "I've got one of theses and youuuuuuu don't!"

So she goes wailing and a crying like she'd just lost her best friend. There was nothing she could do to ease the pain until her mother "shushed" her down with a banana and sent her back outside.

As she takes a big bite of the banana she pulls her panties down, spits out the banana and screams, "My mommy says as long as I have one of these I can get as many of those as I want." Then takes another barbaric bite of her banana.

Penis envy is a math for boys since we can get any size we want, are stuck with the same size we have and have 17 more orgasms than most men can. Unless they know more than, "wham-bam thank-you ma'am."

Even this joke flew over my newly developing intellect and brought new meaning to my understanding of sexual deviance.

I was sexualized the way most little girls are in American society.

I was sexualized by Barbie. It was the mid seventies where you had Barbie and her co-horts but who gave a fuck about them? What was really fun was getting Barbie all naked and Ken comes over in his Hawaiian shirt and caresses her breast. I would wear this lingerie that was popular at the time and with the dream house there was a cocktail shaker and pool outside.

Barbie was entertaining the others and then they just fell to the wayside as we were curious back then with the way Barbie could bend. They fucked up that dream. Not with permanent panties of today that hide the way the lips slid together and give a girl the imagination of a slit between her legs (not knowing where pubic hair is to grow). That's the kind of "Educating Rita" we had as children. That we were never going to develop that nasty hair our mothers had because we're all plastic.

That was also back when Ken was made of plastic and you could kinda sorta see his balls but didn't really get the concept of a cock but that Barbie loved Ken an awful lot.

They would stand together and she would wrap one leg around the hip then he would hold her butt up so they could dance like that. Since Barbie was more of a ballerina during the day at night she became a gymnast.

I learned things from her I used in Tales of the Uncontrollable Cunt where she was flipped back and Ken had her by the hips and she was doing back bends. Then she would set her legs up on his shoulders. After that got boring one of the girls would take Barbie by one leg while another would take the other and then Ken would get in behind them and plow into Barbie.

Now part of this was play acting but a lot of it was being able to peek in on my mother who was 5"4', 111 while my father who was 5"10' had been in the Army and could throw her around like a doll, which he did at least 1x we saw. "Show no bruises." So he would spank her and spank her until she'd wince and begged him to stop, he was going to wake the children.

But the children were all quietly watching and when the door was opened they all went screaming back to their bed not understanding what had just happened and what mommy did to deserve such a hard spanking.

At 15 I would stay in my bedroom wondering what all the fuss was about, not really giving fucks about. I did not want to end up like my parents even though I was already on the pill to regulate my periods.

But it felt just fine giving myself orgasms on a Saturday night listening to the Flip Side on 98.1. But that was first so she could please herself before she was pleased by another.

When we were children we found our mother's cream colored dildo she'd leave under her bed. Under my father's a gun. But her dildo looked like a missle. We called it "the battery tester" because my mother didn't know what to say when we found it.

But I didn't need one of those to please myself since I didn't know what it was. But I knew that by letting my fingers do the walking I was letting myself know who was in charge of my pussy and that even though it felt so wrong touching myself as a Christian it felt so right at the same time.

The next morning I always felt refreshed and alive.

I learned to discipline the feelings I had for myself even though in my past I never wanted to be touched by anybody.

Now I can't touch myself enough even though I wish I could do it more. I hold off for the Bigger Bang for my FUCK . Plus it's so messy I have to put down at least three towels if I want to come once. If I need to come more than that I need to put some kind of waterproof sheets.

By all means, please let me know how it works for you!!!

This article has been ripped off since 1997 however not as extensive as what is written in this book since that was written 25 years ago)

AWAKENINGS

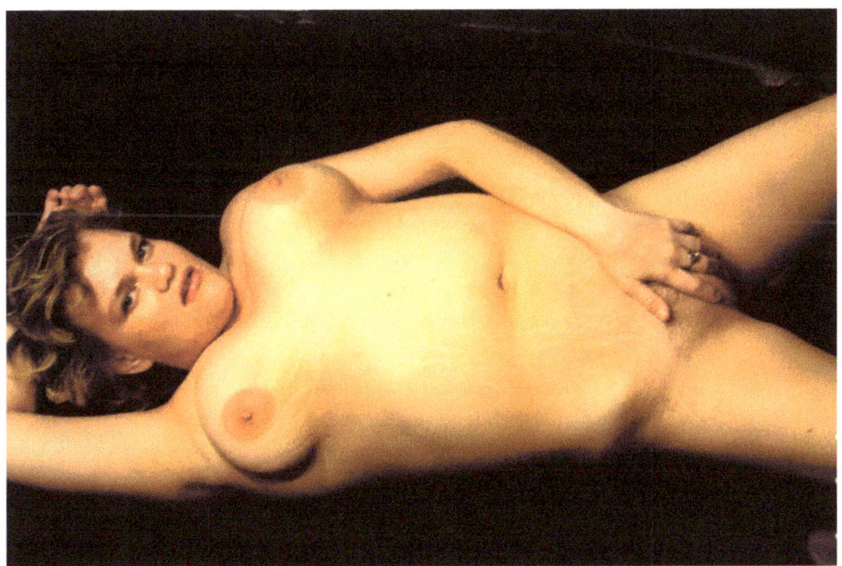

We need to start teaching girls how to be sexualized instead of teaching them to be objectified. A girl's first sexual experience with another person her age is their business. Age APPROPRIATE. Sure people come gossip and stuff about it but let them say whatever the fuck they want we need to teach people how to deal with how we personally sexualized girls in our culture.

Not solving issues by putting plastic permanent panties on Barbie so that we don't see her slit. Bring back the slit! Let's teach girls they have a clit. It's not fun to make Barbie fuck Ken wearing underwear.

The way I played with my Barbies was epic. Backbends with Ken coming up and fucking her... thinking back I was either a precocious child or I had seen things I shouldn't have seen. My guess would be a little bit of both. Especially because I was three when I started to do this.

The first time I'd ever felt a boy's breath against my mouth I was 8. The standard age of most children going back before Rome. I couldn't understand why he wanted me. But it was easy access and I am mildly retarded. I was wearing my green polyester vest suit with a hole in the bottom where the pants were.

Michael wanted to show me this painting that glowed in the dark so he took me into his closet and we started looking at it before his mouth was again on my lips. I didn't know what to think just that it felt like my body was being invaded by lightning bugs and fairies.

He tried to get under my vest to feel her budding breasts but there was nothing @8 because I wouldn't take my shirt off. He couldn't put his mouth on my breasts, just breathe on them like little fires on my nipples.

He undid my green pants with my red flowered panties. I didn't understand what that meant but knew there was another hole in my pants down there. He slowly pulled his penis out and I looked at one up close and personal for the first time. He opened the door just a little so I could see the angry dark purple apple peer back at me. A little fat head he had pinched between 2 fingers. "Do you want to touch it?"

"No."

He put his hand back up my shirt and played with my nipples in ways that I didn't know I could ever feel. We rubbed up and down on each other's hips until we were more scared about getting caught over the carnal pleasures we were both feeling unless he came and I didn't, sardonic. smile..

He gave me a hug and we left his room.

The next day we went back into his closet to look at more glow in the dark art that needed no light and he was just showing me what he made until his mother opened the door and started screaming at us both. I didn't know what to do but screamed over and over, "PLEASE DON'T TELL MY DADDY" praying she would tell my mother until I got home and could cry on HER shoulders.

That Catholic Cunt filled me with enough rage and anger of a non Catholic woman that is forced upon little girls to last me well into my grandchildren's death.

That women had to wait to be touched a certain way until they were married, which confused me since my father was no longer married. Nobody back then got away from that kind of child abuse, not like today. It's just the acceptable way of keeping girls subservient while boys "rule the world". It was the worst experience in my life after moving into a new place with no friends.

I was dirty, and I should never touch myself again. I'd sit in a bathtub and hope that it would get clean and use massive wads of toilet paper so I didn't have to wipe my cunt.

I went home crying and could never love myself again. My sister would tell me how much she would love me and I would tell her to shut up because of what Michael Puckett's mother did to me. Let alone all the child abuse he much have sufferered under that cunt's control.

After that, she was no longer our babysitter and soon moved. I felt like it was all my fault and we never had another babysitter because of what I had done but my father never acted like there was anything I had done wrong. That everything was hunky-dory and I was just simply a chip off the 'ol block.

The light between her legs was what they were always talking about as love. Like when Daddy would slither down the streets as fast and as hot as his Porsche would run watching me in the rear view mirror burn. My poor tutu so I would beg for him to let his princess ride there but because he had to torture his wife's twin just for looking like her he wanted to make her suffer just because he could.

At 10 I had to get naked because the doctor had instructed me. Not EVER wanting to upset my father I did exactly as I was told and put the gown on and told her when I was ready. I sat up on the table that every woman must do, the rite of passage. Seeing the gyn for the first time.

Nobody asked her mom if she wanted a doctor to look at her, but her child was violated. Another way he loved to fuck with me as a child without fucking me as a child. Mom had been teasing me about the newly emerging discharge as being an STD, Stinky Tutu Discharge, which was THE beginning of the biggest rite of passage.

After the nuclear disaster of what he did to their family my mother had to have a boarding house to save it so we could have a place to live, plus she had built it for her prince and princesses but daddy had to worship his cock.

My father, mean old Mr. Tooth Decay, decided to take me without even bothering asking me if anyone had ever touched me and naturally assumed I would lie because that was the kind of child he convinced me I was after the time I called CPS on him because I was scared of being alone with my brother and my daddy came home, screamed at me and beat me that I was never to lie like that again, hence separating the pieces that lie into his truth and the pieces that lie in my subconscious like the precious memories that are mine (finally off fentanyl understanding that he was a Coke head his work had more meaning) .

The heat from the lamp was warm and felt nice but what happened next was worse than any horror story I had ever experienced in my entire life. It was like a scene from, "**Sybil**." The doctor started touching me in ways nobody had ever touched me and I just started wailing because my father wouldn't let my mother be there and it wasn't like anyone else was there for me except the secretary that broke my parents up, the secretary he wouldn't let have his child as a good little girl she listened to Daddy too. He didn't want a child to spoil her figure.

She used both the fingers then slid the coldest, wettest device inside me to make me think this was not a place to touch. This was not a place that was sacred.

This place never belonged to me even though it was a part of my body. It was when I learned that every woman had to take it and every man was the one to give it to me.

It was the first day of 10th grade and I had missed it. It was either a Monday or a Wednesday it didn't matter because it was light years away before I would be in my mother's arms crying about what had happened and she would python love all the hate I held inside of me

It left her feeling trepidation of the entire male population as the minor pleasures of my brain would elicit feelings of romantic joy. A back rub for her father and uncle. The way I would kiss one of the boys in the boat house.

Feeling that feeling made me feel visceral. That my body was never going to belong to me but rooms inside pieces of my mind that even I couldn't reach they were too raw to show.

If you don't think I don't know her, she's typing with her fingers knowing this violation that happened to me as a child as I'm finding out my father is the Pablo Escobar of Kentucky I can get it.... Yeah I can see how a fucking Coke head could think this was no big deal.

A walk in the park.

What I can't seem to come to grips with is the Louisville Bar Association allowing my father to continue to practice knowing he was a cokehead and took his little Porsche away yet left him the custodial parent of three children.

WTF??

What is blowing my mind right now is how many adults got together to make this decision not to take this man's license away?

Did you not know that he took my mother to Court 67 times? And he would do it when he was delivering Coke.

I should have some great instructional videos on early YouTube no gwt off on *CatherineClay.Com*

MY FIRST CRUSH

Sweet memories to behold about my father. At least ONE. I had my first crush on CH. During   South Oldham Middle School in Crestwood, Kentucky.

I used to just look at him and his goofy, nerdy wearing polo shirts all the time. I finally started stealing my father's when I was in Middle School because he never dressed us. We were useless counts so everybody thought we were poor.

So I would look at him and history and I would look at him in English and I would just look at him and watch him in All His Glory.

He has an aunt named Jane and she was one of the first most wonderful people in my entire life (and I hope she friends me) in middle school because she actually turned me in when I tried to kill myself. When I was 13. My dad wouldn't pay for my makeup subscription and yelled at me for getting it. Yelled at me for a lot of fucked up things but I still love the fucker... but now that I can think I wrote this before I knew so many things he does I abhor but this is the one positive thing he did in my life. (sorry but mom put a roof over our head, clothed us but couldn't feed us because you took that honor away. Then put locks on the door so food can only stay at your place instead of nourishing us on the weekends like we needed. But we were possessions just like your food.)

My Dad figured out I had a crush so he smiled and thought it was cute so he bought me some **Polo** cologne for me to give him for Christmas. I opened it and put it on to tease him and everybody else. I was quite the seductress even in Middle School.

He splooged when he found out daddy drove a Porsche.

I fucking loved riding in that thing when we got to ride in it. Even though my dad made me ride on the hump so that my vagina burned every time we would drive for a little bit.

And he used to go *fast*. There is this turn in one of the ways to get onto the freeway in downtown Louisville that moves with a big semi circle. Whenever we would come home from his office we would go up at and it always felt like a fucking roller coaster

I was bummed that we never went to Danville or I am bummed that we never did. We used to go to Danville to go to the lake house and naturally I rode the hump but they have wheeee hills. It was so much fun to just lose your stomach and have those butterflies that you get from riding really fast.

When the Gene Snyder freeway first opened up my Dad drove onto the freeway with us in the car and we went as fast as he could take us all the way through. Just the 4 of us. It was so beautiful. Before the eyesores took root, they were always there until they turn to soot.

I think Britney came home with me one time in it and a few other friends that I have so they were *privileged.*

My dad had a magazine about Lamborghinis and other flying cars I think and I brought it to show my crush. He ended up working for Porsche.

The Louisville Bar Association discovered that Porsche was bought with Blood Money so they made him get rid of it however they left us in custody with him knowing what kind of person he is, was and always will be. An emotional invalid.

I had this nasty doctor use both fingers then slide the coldest, wettest device inside me making me scream, teaching me this was not a place to touch. It was not sacred. This place never belonged to ME even though it was a part of MY body. It was where I learned that every woman had to take it and every man was the one to give it. The legacy in which my father left me with.

It was the first day of 5th grade and I'd missed it. It was Monday, light years away before I would be in my mother's arms crying about how my father had molested me using a doctor instead of just asking me if I had been molested. She knew what had happened and she would python love all the agony I held inside of me.

It left me feeling trepidation for the entire male population as the minor pleasures would elicit feelings of romantic joy.

A back rub for my father and uncle. The way I kissed one of the boys in the boat house. Feeling my awakening made me feel visceral. That my body was never going to belong to me but rooms inside, pieces of my mind that even I can't see memories too raw I can't reach.

I found myself while listening to **Sonic Youth's PCH** racing down in the covers wondering. Feeling all I could think of making my own fireworks go off in my head but it was reserved for tantalizing delights I was not ready to share. I was 15 and mentally aware with my own room to finally figure myself out.

The first time I was aware I was different down there was not with the baths that I shared with my brother, even though my mother irritated the story of when I "returned from the hospital someone cut off my tinker," my brother cried his little mind blown that not everybody had a penis large enough to show. They gave me a gift.. The gift of being female.

Nor was it the time my neighbor, in my discoveries where my neighbor would pull his pants down, in the sand yard as my panties were moved to the side.

My favorite joke always goes with this little cocksucker pulling his pants down and screaming "I've got one of theses and youuuuuuu don't!"

So she goes wailing and a crying like she'd just lost her best friend. There was nothing she could do to ease the pain until her mother "sushed" her down with a banana and sent her back outside.

As she takes a big bite of the banana she pulls her panties down, spits out the banana and screams, "My mommy says as long as I have one of these I can get as many of those as I want." Then takes another barbaric bite of her banana.

Penis envy is a math for boys since we can get any size we want, are stuck with the same size we have and have 17 more orgasms than most men can. Unless they know more than, "wham-bam thank-you ma'am."

Even this joke flew over my newly developing intellect and brought new meaning to my understanding of sexual deviance.

I was sexualized the way most little girls are in American society.

I was sexualized by Barbie. It was the mid seventies where you had Barbie and her co-horts but who gave a fuck about them? What was really fun was getting Barbie all naked and Ken comes over in his Hawaiian shirt and caresses her breast. I would wear this lingerie that was popular at the time and with the dream house there was a cocktail shaker and pool outside.

Barbie was entertaining the others and then they just fell to the wayside as we were curious back then with the way Barbie could bend. They fucked up that dream. Not with permanent panties of today that hide the way the lips slid together and give a girl the imagination of a slit between her legs (not knowing where pubic hair is to grow). That's the kind of **"Educating Rita"** we had as children. That we were never going to develop that nasty hair our mothers had because we're all plastic.

That was also back when Ken was made of plastic and you could kinda sorta see his balls but didn't really get the concept of a cock but that Barbie loved Ken an awful lot.

They would stand together and she would wrap one leg around the hip then he would hold her butt up so they could dance like that. Since Barbie was more of a ballerina during the day at night she became a gymnast doing impossible human capabilites. Especially when she could move her legs around.

I learned things from her I used in **Tales of the Uncontrollable Cunt** where Barbie was flipped back and Ken had her by the hips and she was doing back bends. Then she would set her legs up on his shoulders. After that got boring one of the girls would take Barbie by one leg while another would take the other and then Ken would get in behind them and plow into Barbie.

Now part of this was play acting but a lot of it was being able to peek in on my mother who was 5"4', 111 while my father who was 5"10' had been in the Army and could throw her around like a doll, which he did at least 1x we saw. "Show no bruises." So he would spank her and spank her until she'd wince and begged him to stop, he was going to wake the children but Tsk, we heard we saw you threaten our mother.

But the children were all quietly watching and when the door was opened they all went screaming back to their bed not understanding what had just happened and what mommy did to deserve such a hard spanking.

At 15 I would stay in my bedroom wondering what all the fuss was about, not really giving fucks about. I did not want to end up like my parents even though I was already on the pill to regulate my periods.

But it felt just fine giving myself orgasms on a Saturday night listening to the **Flip Side** on 98.1. But that was first so she could please herself before she was pleased by another.

When we were children we found our mother's cream colored dildo she'd leave under her bed. Under my father's gun. But her dildo looked like a missle. We called it "the battery tester" because my mother didn't know what to say when we found it.

But I didn't need one of those to please myself since I didn't know what it was. But I knew that by letting my fingers do the walking I was letting myself know who was in charge of my pussy and that even though it felt so wrong touching myself as a Christian it felt so right at the same time.

The next morning I always felt refreshed and alive.

I learned to discipline the feelings I had for myself even though in my past I never wanted to be touched by anybody.

Now I can't touch myself enough even though I wish I could do it more. I hold off for the Bigger Bang for my BUCK . Plus it's so messy I have to put down at least three towels if I want to come once. If I need to come more than that I need to put some kind of waterproof sheets.

RAPE

Quit feeling so alone, you goddamn pussy. You dumb cunt. You were asking for it, begging on all fours, were you? Weren't you?

So far my favorite compliment as a writer came from a woman who been sexually abused by her stepbrother. The Admiral in the Navy got in touch with me to tell me that his wife went through dark phases when he couldn't reach her. Then she read **Tales of the Uncontrollable Cunt** and "her dark phases got fewer and far between. Do you have more books she can read?"

"That's just the second of around 16 Volumes." Nothing has made me feel better than keeping this and my pocket for those rainy days where I feel worthless.

Well in order for a girl to become a woman she is raped. She learns that her body is not her own and what was once a whole human soul on her own accord she now understands that she has to take it Leica man.

Catherine's Rules to being a Sexist Cunt back.

#1 How can I, Miss CATHERINE ELIZABETH smirking mother fucking CLAY, have penis envy when I can get any size I DEMAND?

This MIGTF, Mother I get to fuck?
(Next to Russian I've found Englush to be so... banal. So flat {water dripping out of my mouth as I say it}... We don't have "wrapped in a cunt" and "fucked by a dick" no... so from now on I'll just Patsy (my mom) myself on the back.

My favorite joke you have to hear in Russian to understand is that a friend asks another friend to go to the doctor and he say, no no thank you but I'm either "Hue(y) ova"{dewey and Louie's. Ducks, Dicks, in a row} or "piz-detz" {wrapped in a cunt} and if I'm "Hueova" I can fix it myself but if I'm "piz-detz" I'm really fucked.
"IF you don't have your health you have nothing to lose.... but humor and are dissed to become abled")

1. no one took the man from woman
2. no one took the he from she
3. no one took the male from female.
4. no one took the God from Goddess
5. women create life therefore we are gods walking in our own image of ourselves while men... have to walk in their "God's" He's not YOURS. Quit giving the invisible cock the power he does not deserve however tap into the collective consciousness to know when you are right within yourself.
6. men are known to take off so some men are men some men are fathers and the rest of us are mothers. Quit thinking you're not a man.

7. The Bible is a blasphemous fucking trashy rag of pulp fiction of earlier men's inferior abilities playing superiority complexes. The only redeemable chapter is the "Song of Songs"

8. women aren't better than men we are all men it's just... we get to have more orgasms so I guess, yeah, that makes us superior to Ys.

9. "You are beautiful in every single way" don't let rape bring you down

10. If all men are created equal why are you bitching about illegals taking up space?

11. You do not need to traffic yourself for love. Quit giving your love away to a man that can not love himself therefore will never learn how to love you no matter how unconditionally he gives of himself.

12. You have a right to be a pussy since you have a pussy and know what that truly entails just like you can never think outside the box you reside in.

13. All men eat their cum and wonder why if they don't have a problem with it then why should you? And if you ejaculate and say, "Baby can I cum on your face" most men don't have a problem with it.

14. You are always the youest you and I'm always my meest me.

15. I was born blonde but grew out of it. You can too.

16. Divorce Miss Clairol. She's not doing your brain any favors

17. All brain tumors are not created equal. *acyst.org* me

18. At one point in your life you are going to be dissed to become abled. Don't look a gift horse in the mouth to change yourself to be a better you.

19. to be raped is learning how to let the past you die while the new you learns how to thrive fuck surviving.

20. You are never safe. You can not protect yourself but luckily there is social media to help end it all. I know. I'm an OG framer of this all.

Take it Leica Man. I do.

Your body is never whole again yet a XY's body is once you take him in. Funny that I've been thinking about XY and XX as XX and Ys for years. Before trans was acceptable. Because no matter what you identify yourself to be your sex is your sex. Quit wearing yours so awkwardly.

Rape... it's how women have been introduced to life since for millenniums. We were Atom's bones made of leukemia. That men are better than us because **WE** shove that goddamn Apple down Adams throat. Don't take responsibility for your own goddamn actions but Blame It On a Woman because that's what Society does. We are the fairer sex, we just don't get sex the way a man does. We don't have the "sex drive a man does." I :}}} can have 18 types of orgasms and Josh :{}}} got up to 5. Wham Bam, slow release, no release, anal, oral. Oh he had the sweetest ass to fuck. Sticking a vibrator up his ass and keeping it in with my feet as his cock vibrated inside of me... I'm patiently waiting for the man to do the impossible and find my grandmother's ring.

All women are supposed to have rape fantasies when I, personally, after speaking to millions of women in my almost 50 years do not WANT. It's something it's just something we have EXPERIENCED and get to live with on a day to day basis on some fucking level.

Starting as a little girl. Targets on our backs. The prettier the less self confidence. The easier a Mother's boyfriend's raping hands find their way in your coat making you feel so *SPECIAL {"the church lady" SNL clip}

If you are being raped and you want it to stop start acting like you're enjoying it. It will scare a man trying to frighten you just as laughing at my dad when I was 15 for his flying Ninja spank me moves on my ass for losing 5 polo shirts, a GA shirt that cost over $125 but wouldn't clothe us nor give us money to clothe ourselves and he was laundering Drug Money imagine that. Start what you are trained to do and act. Act like it's getting you off so that it stops because a man that thinks he's hurting you starts feeling like you're asserting you really makes him want it to stop.

You could start laughing at him but that's only if you know the guy. IF that doesn't warp his sense of hurting a woman for the rest of his life then you pulled a bigger number on him than he ever could on you or women he tries to do this to. Please big invisible cock, hear my prayer for my ghouls growing into women to be a **"Roll of Thunder Hear my Cry."**

Starting as a little girl you understand that there is something in between your legs that tells you you are different from others and that through this difference you must hate/envy/greed on other XX. You can't just be mates as Ys are with Ys. But that's a future blog. How Ys feel about Ys. Gen Xers, like baby boomers, are wondering what it feels like to take a cock inside of them. The more ass obsessed the harder he's trying to surpass his obsession with the taste of other cocks. How it must feel to lick the tantalizing mushroom of a head seeing how deep he can really take it in.

I was playing with Alex B as a child showing him mine as he showed me his as he was trapped inside one day. I pulled up my skirt and fainted as he plastered his cock against the window. "Cathy Clay streakier" was a nickname of mine that if you call me one time I will never look your way again.

All that girl on girl porn they've watched most of their lives has left them wondering what's on the other side but will never know whereas women... clicking tongue, we've got your number and you'll never have ours. Or at least I do and will be teaching you.

Women are raped by society from birth. We are torn from wombs most ungraciously realizing it's a cold, cruel word since birth because it starts off being torn away from our mothers. Others have their cocks chopped to further the isolation we all suppress up on someone sometime in our lives. Or in today's society for your entire live... until middle age when it all blows up in your face.

I was introduced to full force rape when I was 17 and my friend told me Derrick Age had raped her. Now everybody doubted her... called her a liar but from the get go I did not. **Date rape** was a concept that was coming on the horizon. I cried like I'd never cried when I found out... HOW DARE HE??? Take the most PRECIOUS THING BORN TO WOMAN, OUR VIRGINITY. Hers and mine both.

Some girls never have the luxury of knowing that much about themselves which leads to a lifetime of deep seeded feelings that your body isn't your own leading to the mind/body split. Kind of like living with the brain tumor you get to age with and if you are kind enough I would appreciate a donation to the arachnoid cyst foundation, acyst.org, because when you live with as other's like to say "benign" brain lesion that fucks your mind up from the get go you learn HOW TO LIVE OUTSIDE YOUR OWN BODY. You don't have a choice or you'll go mad.

RAPE is taking a piece of yourself you do not identify as your own so you take it away from you so that it is not incorporated into your personality such as is masculinity. Just as I have justified my blatant cussing to the carefully contained Tourette's I did not choose to take on I've incorporated it so it is, indeed, a very much part of me even in polite conversation.

It took my "friend" (I don't want to talk to strangers about this) 2 years to tell me. 2 years of fucking torture in not understanding the hatred and loathing I had mirrored at me vs. the sisterly frienderly bonds that should have been growing between us.

Something my father raped from us by divorcing our mother and talking shit about her. Hating on us for simply being "The Girls" unable to carry on the "family name" (which is why I had a bastard since my brother wasn't going to further our dynasty because he is gay.)

"Mommy they cut her tinker off" he whined to my mother our first bath thinking that without one or the sheer horror of it not existing and even understanding that as a baby his cock was chopped, as his own already had been, only completely off scared him that he could do something wrong so they'd turn him into a girl without a cock.

Why men have been so scared of our little cocks they've been cutting them off for millennia to make us more desirable to rape and rape and rape again for the simple freedom to be born a woman. They cut them off to sublimely remind themselves that we all start off with cunts in the womb it's only the flip of a Mother's switch that can reverse a child's sex making some XYs XXs. I learned this from the Berlin Olympics because they wouldn't let a man compete as a man but switched him to a woman because he didn't sex out genetically however physically...

As time wore on, and thinking of this just now, I took a "Sex Crimes" class with PhD. Holmes at UofL and he talked about how serial killers take trophies. They talk about it in SVU, a rape victim's favourite TV show so they can teach her that other women have target's on their backs, too, and that once you're popped XYs can't stop. My best advice, after consuming decades of this show, is to laugh.

That prick that raped my friend Tina my dad's drug dealer's daughter, Derrick, took trophies. Photographs of us growing up together. So not only was he a rapist he would jack off watching her and myself grow up, back when privacy was a habit our children and our children's children will never comprehend. Life before photography was a crime and was an art for in its stead.

Derrick was wanking it thinking of raping her while going back looking at photos of her growing up so he was always a pedophile. When I found out I went ballistic.

I KNEW Tina had been raped because I experienced the brunt end of what it felt like to decimate someone on a daily basis because you have to see their ugly fucking faces and face them in the halls at school and when that mother fucker knew I found out I made it very plain what I was going to do. She sicked me on him like a viper. Punkers, EMOs, "alternative" lifestyles were just coming into play and I was my class favourite's "most individual." A title I shall forever relish as I continue living up to it today.

"You give me those god damn photos back or I'll cut your dick off."

"Is that a threat or a promise?" his fugly face with a comical nose, disgusting breath that is known only as ginger's have (there is a reason we are made fun of and the more ginger fragrant you shall be... to me and select others too), his acne. Stooping down at me I remember every freckle, every acne scar, every sinew growing brighter red as I might as well have been yelling RAPIST vs. the whispering bubble I had created around us.

Him a 6"4' football player's gaze more intense than his experience of someone hating back at him except for the fear he arose in my sister's eyes only other family members had raped from her consciousness, "It's a god damn promise." I say before Tarentino had made Uma his star.

And my fucking POS father billing over a billion against sexual harassers much easier than he was on his clients, army underlings, secretaries least we forget his own "girls", are pet names. Liar.

Tinaa lied about being raped. Or he just wanted to blame a woman undergoing the fight for her life raising 3 fucked up militarized teenagers that finally turned on him for the honor he bestowed of wanting to raise his son alone but taking on the extra baggage. "The Girls" even though I was a boy to grow into a man.

As my father had raped my mother, as Donald fucking Trump has taken teenagers, because they feel it's their right as upper middle class uptight men to be blessed with all of their chosen desires. To steal ours away from us and pervert us into their own image objectifying us so our human rights are not like their own. Making XXs understand and detest all that makes us who we are as people in our own "manifest destiny" images. Being a whole person. Owning your own soul.

In reading **John Berger's "Ways of Seeing"**, a book that switched my light on objectification as I've objectified XYs on their own glaring at them with my own photographer's lens. Then I had the honor of watching his BBC series much later in life on YouTube.

My father raping my mother, that shit lives in your DNA. Your mother, your mother's mother. My grandmother didn't feel sorry for Tina as hers was taken the old fashioned way. Totally and completely away from her as a child. "I thought no good would come of it by the way she'd bounce all over him." But you never told her so. She didn't get it. She certainly isn't the dimest nor the slimist of this branch anymore.

Granny taught me what it meant to be a woman since my mother was too ill to do it alone. That I'm just like any man and put my pants on like most, "one leg at a time." That "my shit stinks just as bad as yours" so I would not feel "better than anybody but I was just as good as every body." My father, being a Clay, felt that it was our birthright, or his and my brother's, to dominate and de-infiltrate class struggles, to each his own.

That as blue bloods the rules do not apply to me much to my chagrin. I make them up as I go along playing my own games to get off and win.

With all these rapes that slowly started to unravel themselves to me it prepared me for something I could never imagine myself to be. My own rapist.

MY FIRST LUST

After I had my first crush it took three years before I felt my first lust. This was long before I learned to gush.

I was 15 and starting a different High School because Middle School everybody was too mean. So I went to school at Boyle County High turning me into a rebel. Everybody had very little skills except when it came to fucking. That's when I learned what butter was good for.

As I walked in the cafeteria door I saw his big blue eyes that were a cross between my sister's deep blue, brother's between the two and Dad's icy gays which should not even phase you, gentle reader.

For a nanosecond I felt my heart pitter-patter then in unison his friends and cried out, "hey baby." Then laughing hysterically to see their reaction on each girl's face to be.

I went from feeling so beautiful and pleasant to feeling like **Carrie** with blood soaked everywhere. Everyone could see how everyone already hated me. I graduated from "scum" to "heifer" then mutated into something I didn't quite understand. Something the boys couldn't comprehend. I was as much a predator as they were prey.

It was a very rough time because everything was uncertain because my mom was dying. I didn't need the extra attention, you see, simply because my breasts were bigger than me.

I was so embarrassed and felt so fat but I never lifted them up to see just how skinny I was. I just have these melons attached to my chest.

They did it again the next day which made me run away so I never ate in the cafeteria again because I didn't have any friends.

As we grew older and began to age we would often wonder what was the next stage of their horrific hormones.

I was being abused and was always confused.

As we grew up I would try to get together but... I chastised him for wanting to keep his hair just like he was young and love to stare like narcissist in the pool to fall never enjoying a satiating sex life at all. I told him it didn't really matter and that vanity was not a blessing to me. I wanted us to take the money and run all the way to Europe with our honeys.

But he had other things in mind and we ended things not very kindly. Fentanyl is a horrible drug that bends your mind and makes you feel like a slug.

Yesterday he friended me and I was so happy just to see all the things that he had to say and was really enjoying my day until I saw the photo that stopped my fluttering heart.

"I told you your hair never mattered." The photo that I'll never forget splattered telling his children that he was dying from stage 3 cancer.

That was over a year ago and I am happy that we can have a little life to be completely in love and oh so sappy. But I dunno, he won't text me back so I must have made him unhappy.

If he's going that way then hey no Clay for Cho at the end of the day saying, "honey I'm glad your home."

It might not be long and he might not be very strong but I just want to be the last woman to make him happy. I've loved him since I was 15 and to have this chance I never thought could be the best and moist and an excited gushy, giggling, girly thing that I'd do to myself just wandering.

I don't care if he's dying as long as he's trying. I can make everything right and stay strong with his might and not lose sight of who I want to be and how deeply I desire him inside of me.

Once Upon a Time he gave me a glance of what he had packing inside his pants. It's worse than the longest, slowest strip tease in history, if you're feeling me. It left me wet and I was set for my husband thinking of another man for the first time in as long as any memory I can because that's gross not to be with who you are at the time you are inside with me.

My desire was so flush I couldn't believe how my pussy gushed just imagining what it would be if his cock was deep inside of me.

I can't remember if I sent him a picture of my cunt or if that was something he'd even want. I can't remember if we jacked off together but I certainly did think of slobbering all over his head. Feeling him kissing my cervix with his cock so deep making me scream like a freak.

He's like the perfect size, not too fat, not too thin but plenty long to get into my uterus and hopefully keep it cumming along.

How I want to lick the mushroom that is the tip of his prick and I don't give a fuck that he is sick. Like I told him the other day, "I just want your cock." I didn't know what else to say. I didn't realize he was loaded and that is why I exploded.

I'm not in the mood for a Tinder fuck so I feel that it's just my luck and I hope he gets stuck so deep inside of my womb that it no longer feels like a tomb.

All I want to do is explode all over in-between his legs. I guess it's a taint making me wonder if I'm just a saint for wanting to feel him so deep inside of me because it's what I want to see.

Yes I think it's truly my luck because he's the one I've always wanted to fuck. From the time that my hormones were stirring within me he was the one I wanted on top of me screaming, singing with such glee.

He's still not texted me back and I don't think it's going to happen. I wish I could make him realize that every moment matters and each one can be better and better. In sickness as in health.

I hope it really makes a difference because I think we can make a living that is if I am spitting.

Here's to romance.

Let's hope he'll take me up on a dance.

What was I thinking? Not a chance.

We'll... at least you have your footnote in a book. I love you all the same, Gregg. Sorry you have to go your way. I wish you could have tried mine. I'll still love you throughout time.

DON'T STAND SO CLOSE TO ME

Our political science teacher had had it. He was past his expiration date and needed to go so he did. His replacement what's one of the most Exquisite MAN I'd ever met and had the biggest hots for teacher but I knew with the way everybody else was that it was never going to be reciprocated.

All the hot little girls would go up to his desk panting like cats on a Hot Tin Roof. It was pretty disgusting to watch them van over each other trying to get his attention. It made me laugh a lot and I would tell him how much it made me laugh when we were together because I was his teacher's aide during his planning period. Amidst all the teachers gave me their test to copy because they knew I wouldn't give them away because other people had to work as hard as I did.

My mother was dying and I felt so unattractive. It was one of the worst times of my life. I never felt attractive because I wasn't thin because my dad told me nobody would love me as long as I was fat. I was stupid enough to believe him.

No I was just a confused teenager with a tyrannical father he loved to call us Liars all the time.

Since I have brain damage I believe them. Or what some of you like to say or like to pretend an injury of your brain can heal because that makes you feel better as a person to think of a brain that can be regenerated. There are some strides but you cannot put myelin sheath back over a nerve. And thoughts traipsing through a brain damage mind on a nerve without protection burns a little. And even though most dumbfucks can't feel their brain I sure AS FUCK can. I hate to be one of those assholes that couldn't tell everybody that you can't when there's something on the root of your nervous system.

I was 17 years old and I had just been diagnosed with a brain tumor. So I wasn't feeling very attractive. I was in such shock because I knew that I was different than everybody else my entire life and I finally had validation that made me feel special that I wasn't making things up any longer. That people couldn't tell me to just "get over it" because they didn't understand what it was like. Not knowing if it was cancer made it rough. Especially on my mom because even though I didn't understand what was going on she did.

When we found out I slapped her on her back and laughed saying, "I told you there was something wrong with me."

To this day I will never understand how awful it must have felt for my mother to hear me laughing about something that has almost killed me so many times. I don't count anymore, almost being 50.

So when we were having a reunion I used to think of how Samantha Alaska would go up to him with her panties all wet being a slutty seductress when I was still a virgin. She was much more mature than me. She was much thinner than me. But she sure as fuck wasn't as hot as I am. She was a baked Alaska all the time. But I was jealous and as soon as I thought of her little panties getting on hot thinking of him I finally looked him up on Facebook.

He played drums for a band and was fit as hell. He was so hot that I could barely breathe when I was around him. I thought he was so beautiful. But I knew I was no match for Samantha. So I didn't even try to go there with him.

I started to talk to him. I giggled about how the girls used to be about him and he giggled back only to tell me that it was me he was always into. He was only 24 but he felt like a dirty old man crushing on a teenager. I wish I had thought about him after I graduated because he was probably one of the ones I would have ended up with. His wife is my age.

And like so many people our age his wife no longer touches his dick. For some reason women are so freaky once they have their children that they don't want to deal with the men. That's why some men go look for other women because you don't know your body and you can't use it to your advantage or get him to use it to your advantage.

But he wasn't the only teacher that was into me. Dr. Daken's wife had MS. I really didn't understand what that meant at the time. It meant for him to go out and have fun with other women because she wasn't able to please him or even walk for that matter. It was still the 90s so people with MS did not have a quality life with much lividity.

I took **Art in Public Places** and was keeping my Dear Demented Diary that I wasn't sure people we're reading but he was one of my "literary voyeurs."

He was so in love with me. The way he would look at me made me feel so special but I didn't realize that he was undressing me with his eyes. I wasn't riding much about sex at the time just about my mother and her struggles with cancer and how she was dying.

When I wrote, "the shoe fell' that was his expression because he kept waiting for it to drop and never wanted it to. He came to my mother's funeral and was one of the most supportive professors I've ever had. I took a different class from him after that but once I was almost graduated he wanted to come over and play.

So I did.

He's probably the oldest man I've ever been with and from diabetes eating his dick he had to **PUMP YOU UP** by using a pump that was located in his balls to get him hard. He had the biggest belly I'd ever seen in my life. Almost like Santa only it didn't look fat it was just round. Some people have fat and loose skin but he was just a jolly old man.

Before we tried to fool around we went on the Bambi walk that started at the Bambi bar all the way down Bardstown Road. He regaled stories from where they could walk all the way down.

It only took me four bars before I had to leave because I was so drunk. I begged mercy and went home.

So we were in my living room with his massive rotund belly, a penis that needed to be pumped (for those of you that don't know diabetes eats your cock so that it no longer rocks or works anymore. So if you love your dick don't get sick) and me naked looking at him going WTF. "I can't be doing this because he is married."

We tried to do 69 and it just wasn't working for me because I couldn't quit thinking of her thinking of what my father did to my mother. I never wanted to be a homewrecker. I think that's one of the most disgusting things you can be as a woman. If a man isn't happy you don't need to be taking him from his family. There are plenty of loose fish in the sea. All you need is the right hook. Or boat or harpoon.

Plus he was so tiny. We were getting busy and I wasn't in the mood to have him inside of me and I was saved by Ma Bell when the DSL man came around because I was so sick of dial-up. This was in 1998.

I loved Dr Daken because he was just that kind of Professor that everybody wanted to have. He was so much fun to be around and his dirty old man gays always made me feel like a prize especially when I knew that gleam in his eyes was for me.

I wish Jeff had been single and I had hunted for him before I left Louisville because our lives are so radically different but I wouldn't be as happy living in Kentucky all my life.

MY 1ST KISSES

My very first kiss was on top of a tractor on Stoess' Farm across the street from my mother's house with his grandson who asked me to give him a kissy, "mwah mwah mwah."

Or it could have been Alex Bumpus when I was really young. I can't possibly remember except for him being sick one day and me lifting up my skirt.

His mother came and shushed me away.

That also happened to be the house where I believe I could have got my brain tumor because I fell off the fence and had a brick in the center of my head. But my brother claims that it was from the Nazi Relic that still had uranium in it that my father brought home from GERMANY. IDRK. (I don't rightly know).

But the kiss that had the greatest impact on me was from Joshua Harris, my 2nd husband. It was around this time of August as I remember best.

I didn't like him at first when I met him in 2002. He was too much of a stinky hippie and I was a punk rock fairy. He kind of disgusted me by his offensive body odor to which I dubbed him "Stinky." I was married and the night we met will forever live in my mind along with the making of a new group of "friends." It was the night I was raped from my home by that French Fuck. Sleeping in my Honda Passport waiting to have brain surgery I was so out of my mind I couldn't think on my own.

We found a boat on which to float until we ended up on the floor of an old woman. That's where Josh gave me my first foot massage the night before I had my second brain surgery, Feb 2, 2003. It took another 6 months before I left my husband.

He'd dumped me on the 3rd St. Promenade in Santa Monica after hitting me and that's when I met the Sniper. I became afraid of him and my photography professor asked me to move in with her step daughter. I was living on Stanley Hills in a Hollywood Hills bungalow just a hop, skip and a jump from the Laugh Factory where I attempted comedy and met my friend Zorba. Some cocks you know not to touch because they are just too big as was his.

I went to a party in Hollywood with Josh's "friends." He put his arms around me and told me he had the secret of not having to iron his shirts and that was to wear them twice. A habit I broke rather quickly. I asked if anybody had a truck and he was the one that piped in and I asked him if he would help me move and he did.

EA Games in Playa Vista was being built and I went from living single to living in a place with a jacuzzi with yet another roommate. It was a warm summer's night when we were hanging out. I had finally moved all my stuff and he'd stop by after work because I was just a hop, skip and jump from him. He started telling me a story of how Kiera, Amahe's daughter, gave him a kiss and he planted one up on me.

I was being a slut at the time having affairs, some one of a kind, even while dating him. I told him I would not settle for just one as we began the beginning of our relationship. "My cunt belongs to me as your cock belongs to you" to which he replied, "fine." My roommate, Dallas, was insane from my torrents of pained screams of infinite pleasure. She so wanted to tell him how he was not the only one. She wouldn't leave the apartment as I brought men over again and again. She was there always just so fucking stagnant.

But Josh... was something special. We went up to my bedroom after that first kiss and I knew that he'd be mine. He had a wicked long tongue and loved servicing me as much as he could. He was finally done and hopped up off of me as if to go home and masturbate just happy to eat what he ate.

I said, "Where are you going? Get over here." When he dropped his drawers I saw something I'd never seen before. The biggest balls that made me say, "OH Mama." They would bounce deliciously so on my ass causing me to have bigger orgasms again and again. I never knew how much my body would ache for his.

When I swallowed his cock whole he moaned with an extacy he'd never known. He went deeper into this deep throat and my secret was years of bulimia. I breathed so slowly as his moans grew slothingly. Past my uvula which would encompass the head of his cock as he grew deeper in. God how I loved eating his cock and through the years he taught me all his secret spots but for this story I didn't know them quite yet.

I always started with a kiss on the very tip moving and slowly encompassing the head in my mouth is how I would take him in. Slowly ever so much more I licked around the head which was made hard from the horrific circumcision done up on him. It was quite a different flavor as I move my tongue around the head so soft in my mouth with the contrast of the harsh outline and very tender skin underneath it.

I tasted his pre-ejaculation knowing he was pretty clean. A geeky boy with a shy grin. No LA woman would be interested in him. But I looked beyond the bucks and just thought of fucks as we began.

I would take him so deep in my mouth and then get his scar stuck in between my teeth which would give such an unusual response between pain and pure extacy did begin. Deeper still down his shaft I moved in my mouth in the most loving way because that was just the way of Catherine Clay. I pumped my hand down as I sucked, stopping to say, "You've got a big cock" which over time grew much bigger.

Resistance training is different from Kegels, which are more pleasurable just for him. But pushing down is there the action that makes men shout, "let me in let me in let me in."

As he slid into me I squirted rather quickly from practicing my craft of female ejaculation by giving men lessons on how to find it. Is it prostitution when you show a guy a trick and let him just play with your pussy over and over again? I never fucked them, just showed them my trick which Josh was most fond of. After a lesson he'd come fuck the shit out of me but then again I'm jumping the game.

I remember that weekend so intently. Our first that will never end as our energy suspends up on that moment in tyme. I don't know if we ate but we must have drank and got out of bed only to shower, shit and shave. Night turned to day and day rolled into night. We were separated for moments, if that. His refractory period was so impressive I knew I'd hang on to him.

"I didn't know I could do that," he said at his tender age of 31. "It's worse than when I was a teenager." He'd always walk around with half a chub waiting for me to just whistle for 14 years. I don't know how we came back together to go back to work that Monday morning before one more shag even though sleep was unnecessary in this cloud-like dream.

We picked back up the next day. And the day after that until

finally he was the only one in my bed much to my Thai lover, Puman Cho's, chagrin, asking me what Josh had that was not him. I didn't want to give either of them up but I was over being with someone Fresh Off the Boat and using me for all that I'm worth. Plus Josh was so very, very American. A Burbank Boy I never wanted to get involved with. Nobody approved of our union from the get go but they soon learned they didn't have a choice in the type of woman that would pass as the love of his life.

I loved him from the moment he entered my body and our souls united. We were both so pure and exquisitely inviting. Everything he'd been before I turned him into a man seemed discolored and unfulfilling. All his stories of past lovers brought on horror after horror making him fucking miserable.

The warmth of my cunt was something so soft and inviting. He moaned that way that you should whenever you enter somebody else's body turning all my nerves into tendrils of loving precision. Scratching his back was one of the vows I can remember as we married each other in Fantasy Island. He loved the feel of my fingers moving across his back in a hasty precision.

The way the water moved over our bodies as we showered and discovered a new way to fit in each other standing up he was the best fuck. My leg in his arms as I felt his charms enter into me. Laughing a little, this look in his face so intently staring locked into my eyes as if this was the last vision to see which was how it would fatally end up being. Kissing while breathing through water, my back against the wall as his face moved through the head of the shower. Every drop of water that moved with us in a succinct cadence moving through our bodies entwined. I took the Plexion soap and washed away the old man face he was forced to sport.

"Your parents never took you to a dermatologist?"

"No." but they always had time for his brother. The gaps in his teeth always bothered me until with tyme it began to disappear. Self conscious of this he rarely showed his pearly smile, always happy his brother could be cared for better than him but feeling the pain of not being the same.

I always knew what it was like to be second fiddle as well.

I had to stop his beautiful cock as that first time his bushy blonde tufts were like a brillow pad making my shaved, wet skin hurt from them. I took out a razor and oh how I shaved him. Shaving it all off made me feel gross seeing a shaved cock made me feel creepy inside but was a necessary whim. Nestled inside that native bush he would shave off revealed this large dimple like in his chin. This little hole allowed my fingers and my Pocket Rocket to help assist in our dalliances of learning the intricacies of one another's bodies.

It was much easier to learn as I knew where to guide him. He never realized he had a massive cock that only grew stronger and more powerful as we spent so much time **resistance training.**

I remember him in a way other people could only dream of. The sex life we shared nobody really seemed to care for for it was  not happening to them . Once we were together there was no stopping our love as it grew into a family.

Had I known that first kiss from Kiera would make another form of life I don't know if I'd done what I did but Him on top of me, me on top of him, however briefly. Missionary would change as he'd pick me up in his arms so tender and strong I would latch on to my Josh. I would walk up his chest to slam myself down on his cock in total unrelinquished sexuality as our sensuality colored our lives. I slowly washed away the old man whose eczema had stained his face for so many years before me. The red angry face most people had grown accustomed to transformed and noticed quite quickly.

That first time our lives came to rhyme on mysteries, life loves to expand. Days turned to months as months transgressed into years.

That first weekend will never leave me as I learn all the things I'm designing. Let these be the words that some of you have heard and keep in life. Although most people wait to know someone great I was the type to fuck 'em and leave them. But I knew if a man could captivate my attention sexually I would always live with a part of him. Some women wait for the sissy test to take but if you can't get your freak on the first time then your bodies will never rhyme with wit, depth and freedom.

I knew what I was buying that fateful first time as his skills as a web architect swiftly moved faster than mine in the blink of my eye. I latched on because I knew I'd found all my power and my true to life soul mate. Up until this moment I thought it was bullshit but there he was in the flesh, such a boy. Until death did we part but I knew from the start that the energy seeping through our skin would keep finding these rooms I do live in. Much larger than walls that can't hold these thoughts as I take another breath in.

I miss you baby with all of my heart as you brought me such joy by just being a boy and giving me one in your stead. I wish you were here but I could not write with you here. As I write these words with my eyes sealed shut as the tears pour down my cheek. I don't know how I could find someone so meek to my lighting streak as furiously as I took each day as the end for me. Never doubting that you'd always win in the game of life you were cheated from so much more than you'd give.

The ghosts of Christmas past are slowly creeping in as I knew all the love that we shared was but a venner except when it was just the two of us until you knocked me up and we were three. We had to close the door on #4 because we had Jr and our second child was a girl that made me so sick but I so wanted it but you wanted me to be a better mother to Cassius. So many things I would rearrange if I knew what set the stage we were in and how it'd all come to an end of your corporeal existence.

I can feel how we'll meet again but I miss you so much and your oh so gentle touch with your "alligator" skin's touch. I wish you'd listened to me and quit eating so much fucking bacon that broke your heart as well as so many people feel the deep loss of your living.

Letting you in was my greatest sin because you didn't understand how I'd break your heart watching me suffer again and again. But keeping me out without even a shout was your vanity creeping in. You had to keep face, always a saving grace for us and not them. They'll never know so I'll just have to show how life is for the living.

Merry Christmas baby. You taught me to quit living to die so I live to thrive so deep inside and I'm sharing all this with you. Bearing my soul as to fill this empty hole and influence social media again.

Bless your life and all that strife.

"I love you" were the last words you did utter for me and not any of them. I live with this comfort as you know I will love you forever and always... as long as you love me.

MY FIRST BJ

It was Dec of my 15th year and finding other punkers was a rarity in Oldham County, Kentucky. It was a new wave, a new Era of "alternative" lifestyles where we were redefining "the Rules" not always chiming to the tune of mainstream media propaganda.

I was friends with Jesse Meers and she was dating an ugly, older bloke named Scott and he brought his friend just an everyday Joe whose life I turned around again and again my most envious sins I committed with him. Jesse was the embodiment of capricious. I know most Gemini women are noted to be, such as themselves & I am right there with them. Marylin Monroe's Birthday.  Everything was so dramatic with her I couldn't stand it.

Josh around 04 when we first got together before he grew huge and meaty after 12 years of resistance training. Look down to see)

When We Started

Identify regular Joe and I was so excited to know him. "You'll never spend another Friday night alone." he assured me three weeks later. He would come spend those nights at our house of delights, 6416 Hwy 329 Crestwood Ky. 40014 if you'd like to Earth it. It was a scary mansion up on a hill with it often being a dark and stormy night inside a 6400 sq ft box and a horrible upkeep. Cobwebs abound, wafts of cat piss

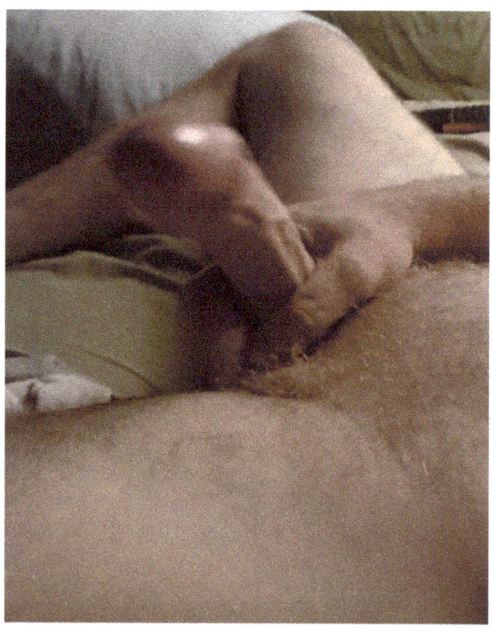

and shit from the dining room as you'd enter the kitchen with an island and a bay window overlooking a creek.

My room overlooked the paddock out back so I'd watch the horses go their own way around as the sun would go down. I don't remember my first kiss but I had my eyes open once to which he didn't like and opened his eyes to make me close mine real quick. It was something else to let him touch me in ways I'd only touched myself.

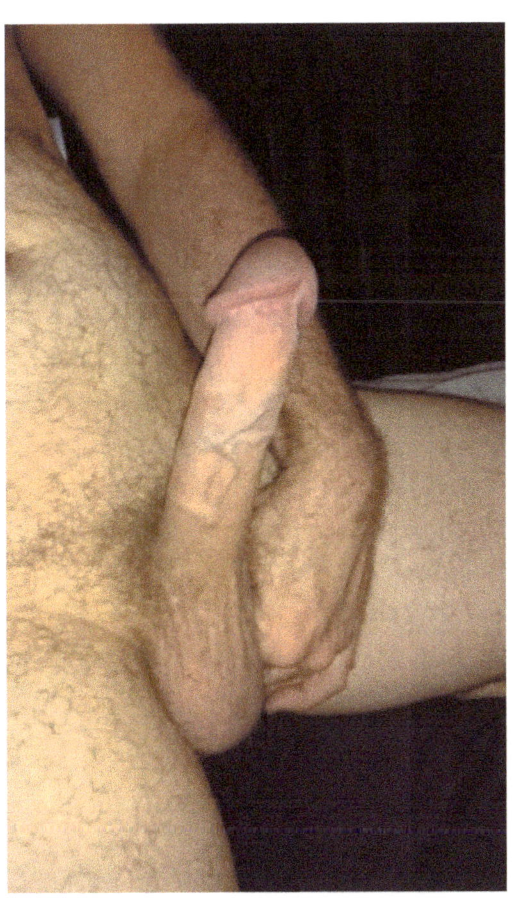

He was experienced, which I didn't like, because his former girlfriend lingered on to his cock like a rock. It was rather big but I didn't know it at the time because it was the first penis I'd ever seen. We'd dry hump a lot in my room back then as I would take him in so privately into my boudoir. It was a lush weekend when we could drum up the cash for my mom to throw us a little bash because life took an edge with her dying. It was something my father used to do as a teenager as well as drink and drive so it was something she was used to.. Abandoned as well from our 8 years of hell that's what my life was about to be that May.

But this was a November to remember as I was still living with the patriarchy. Mom was re-diagnosed with cancer and I slowly took it in as she had to start chemotherapy. He asked Joe point blank, "What are your intentions towards my daughter." as he had knocked up my mother at this age and knew what it was all about.

Everyday Joe was aghast at the accusation that passed as his dick was cut off in that moment. The fear he kept dear as my father was a famous lawyer by then as well as a drill Sergeant with muscles and a tan that defied every other man.

He begged me one day to blow him away and I did because I was bulimic. I studied it but not too close and I'd been jacking him off and I don't remember all the gory details I just remember it being soft to my lips. It didn't last long, this much I do know because our feelings were that of teenagers. I didn't want to fuck and run but wake up to him next to me the next day as we languid would lay but that was not to be a part of our life right then.

The affair led into December and as I write these words on New Year's Eve, when I cried with heaves as Joe had left me for someone that would put out because he couldn't wait until I was 16 to win the "virgin bet" with my mom. $50 was worth the wait to me. We would dry hump to get off and oh my god how did he feel so very fucking real as our jeans turned into just underwear. That was in 1988 and as crazy as my memory serves me I remember the details of my teenage awakening of what wasn't to be.

 Days moved on as my lovelorned heart moved about trying to just "get over it." As years finally passed he emailed me alas as I was traveling through the Ukraine. 10 years had gone by when he found me. I wrote to him naughty as I was so horny from the pure energy that was about from our trip through Kazantip and the in a disabled nuclear Reactor.

He had gotten married to a very scary, often hairy relationship. He was a Networking genius. I knew what that meant. She decided to beat him with a harddrive none the less and he showed up to my place a total mess bleeding everywhere.

That was when I lived on St. James Ct. and it was such a romantic spot when you looked out and about at how Louisville had started all lit out. I mounted him right then, feeling my sin wash over me in waves of desire as I did at 15. It was like fucking a board and he didn't know how to make out what we did it was over quick and I wasn't the right fit. Unrelinquished teenage angst from being left again as he went back to his wife the next day.

Having sex with him wasn't a win/win as I scared him as well. I was hoping to break the cycle of domestic violence but he wouldn't take my hand. I got him a job in Chicago and he brought her up there but I didn't care. It didn't take much longer until it was over.

That fucking prick... used me what a dick.

Now he has a family with a cunt wife that I introduced him to after we reconnected later once again. That being said I had to blow it too just like her husband did after their daughter died because she was a crazy jealous Ukrainian in it for his affection.

Last I heard the fuck wad works for Google. Some people aren't grateful for where you put them and my first love was a dove and flew far far far away from me with glee.

I know he still thinks of me as they all look me up on Facebook and want to fuck or be my friend because I gave them a slice of pie. They always find a way to stray back into my life and say one fateful day, "I should have married YOU."

No fuck but you didn't. Tough luck.

As I stated earlier in this article you should see Josh's cock when he died after 11 years of resistance training this is how much bigger his cock blocked.

I HAD THE TIME OF MY LIFE

This photo is Jr Prom. Not Sr.

I was supposed to take Kirk but he was late and told me he couldn't go then could. My best friend, Lisa Stotts RIP, convinced me to go on a blind date. It was awful. I hated him. My dress is to die for. I've worn it on many special occasions. It's bright red with a sweetheart neckline and fringe. My grandmother made it to fit me perfectly when I was a big girl.

He wouldn't dance, he didn't want to stay and I saw everyone I wanted to see. I'd been on Homebound, school at home because of my brain tumor you get to age with was bothering my thinking.

Won't you acyst me? Nobody cheered for me because I was strong and lasted so long.

I had a photo with my favorite teacher who had the hots for me. I didn't know this until much later that I was the girl "**Don't Stand So Close to Me**." I was enthralled when I discovered this at a much later date. He wasn't much older than me but I still wasn't 18. God I wish I had been with him.

We went to Chris's apartment. He got comfy and I don't remember if I had clothes but Lisa was with me and then she went away.

I blew him and it was ok. Nothing to write home about. He was the second cock I'd ever met and I was not interested in losing my virginity with someone I didn't love. I was old fashioned that way. Call me strange, it's not so much like this today.

But he flipped me over on a bean bag chair and stated a longing stare before he'd gone nowhere a man had gone before. I didn't know what to think as he did sink deeper inside of me. He did this to me and I wasn't thrilled. It was the first time I'd been serviced with enthusiasm. I did not cum. I didn't know about ejaculation yet and the experience was so foreign I couldn't get off.

I wouldn't fuck him right then and there because I wanted someone that cared for me as I cared for him. He was sorely disappointed and didn't call me after so I was glad I didn't let him pop my cherry.

LIKE A VIRGIN

I was a virgin until I was about 21. I was raised foot washing Southern Baptist, which meant no sex before marriage. I realized at 8 that something wasn't great about my cunt. Reading "Truly Tasteless Jokes" taught me that I had a cunt, couldn't get rid of it and was stuck with it forever even though I was a double entendre "Tom Boy". I wasn't growing up. Ut-uh not me. Ignorant of what was going to be a WOMAN!

As a virgin, sex grossed me OUT. Babies, I'd rather puke one out! My mom was pregnant by 16 and told us how she tried to use a coat hanger up her cunt to deliver her baby, because abortion was illegal she had part of the procedure done then half way through put her in an elevator and made her walk for the second ring around. "They could tell what it was." If she only knew how to use her cunt she never would have been stuck with a runt.

"What?" her long silence... finally understanding it was something I would never be a prized son for my dad to see. I was supposed to be a boy but was a wanted child yet was more boy than my brother (I wrote this before I found out he was gay 2020). Always have always will be. More daring, adventurous and caring I would lead and he would follow. I didn't understand why she cried so much watching "**Sophie's Choice**" (**OUAT** was my favorite movie) and what it meant until I became a mother and boy that Sexism is just in our DNA. Listening to her talk about what it was like to be in love and then seeing my sister raped made me hate men. Scared from who my father had been.

I had friends that were boys, most were gay and if not I thought of them that way. I made it through my teens and chemistry. There were a few. Gregg, Sean, Dwayne, Ken, Jeff (hot for teacher), Joe, Brandon, Robbie and Bobbie

(Stop the press... I went to middle school with Bobby Wayne. Then he left and we ended up meeting again when we were working for **Village 8.** He was always stopping me and saying to me, "let me touch your titties."

I don't think this level of sexism exist quite as it did before because women in the 90s didn't know how to tell men to go fuck themselves.

So one day I was signing out when the motherfuker was coming in. He came up behind me and reached around putting his hand on my shoulder and as it started to slide down towards my left tit and said, "let me touch your titties" in such a romantic manner.

Me, being the rancid cunt that I am, said, "OK! You first!" And before he could get even off of my shoulder I reached around and grabbed his dick. It was so hilarious to watch him get as pale as a ghost when the tables were turned. This is what you do to some prick who is sexually harassing you. You put them in their goddamn place.) from Village 8 and the projectionist I wouldn't have sex with. Why? Why does a guy have to ask? Because you know you have a little cock?

I avoided teenage sex successfully. (Only fucked a teenager bringing in 2020.) I got into college and met this boy with long curly hair who was impressed with himself. In a band, talking about a girlfriend. He got me to go up to the golf course where Brownsboro Rd and Frankfort intersect. He asked me to blow him so I did then asked me to go further and I scoffed and wouldn't. I'd just really met him but had seen him around.

I walked into the Quad and there looking up at me was my friend from high school, Andy. Our romance began for 6 weeks of courting. But we later found out we played T-Ball and we're sporting side by side in the photo. He'd taught me chemistry and helped me through the worst times of my life. Giving me self confidence and valuing me when I couldn't. But I'm skipping ahead.

We saw a movie that had a "Woobie" (a security blanket) in it after high school let out and I was between graduating and brain surgery. He never called me back so I didn't think He was interested but that's because he has Asperger's too. Andy made me laugh when my mom was dying but didn't understand the **Full Monty** until we started dating.

It was a six week long courtship before I'd fuck him. I wanted to prepare myself even though I was almost 21. We read about sex voraciously at **Hawley Cooke** trying to discover the many ways to be lovers. I wasn't as intent on that as I was learning about female ejaculation. It intrigued me because I thought it would be fun to cum as boys do.

The first time I remember having sex I had Andy find my g-spot and do what the book had said and just rub and rub and rub all over it. For what seemed like an eternity of waiting and just fumbling around that added to my sexual frustration.

I finally just said, "GET IN!!!"

In about two pumps a tickle and a squirt later I screamed, "DID YOU JUST CUM ON MY ASS???" I had taken the short ride a few times so I knew once he blew a load it was over.

"No," he answered, looking at me in earnest.

He mounts me again and it happens again. I pushed him out with my cunt from having an orgasm and SPLASH he came out again. It slowly dawned on me at the third pump it worked!!! I just kept looking up in the sky feeling deeply, "my oh my" was THAT a real "thing" that women can do to level the playing field?

I remember being so fucking happy that a new chapter in my love life and exploring myself through my journey was opening up a different path than I saw others choosing. However I was also raised believing you were supposed to marry a virgin and stay true blue. Through thick and thin back again but my eye started to stray. I was steadfast for five years (two I spent agonizing how to leave because he'd been there for me after my suicide attempt) until I was just so sexually frustrated I blew some steam off in Europe in 1997.

My mom said she wanted to write a book titled, "It will never be Sunday again." so she wouldn't have to take us back to the monster's house. She is the reason you are reading the words below. Looking through *CatherineClay.Com/censor* you will see what kind of art I was doing about this time and how female circumcision perplexed my mother because she had just had a few lovers in her life, didn't talk much about sex (even though she was a sex kitten up 'til the end) and didn't date. She couldn't even see after Domestic Violence was through with her how she was better off and fairy tales are awesome until you close the book.

I am POSITIVE she would be a little freaked out about the content of my work but I am genuine and "writing what I know" in earnest. I know this doesn't belong here but it tiz. Welcome to the palace of my mind unlocking chapters hidden within while others just be left behind.

I loved being a late bloomer. I made a deal with "God" that I couldn't die a virgin so that's why I knew I was going to live through my first brain surgery. I just didn't expect the last brain surgery to have caused me so many problems but you never know what you're going to get when you're suffering from an "injury."

MELISSA

Melissa and I worked @ **Village 8** together. She was awaiting her nursing license and biding time. I was working there because my mom's 2nd residence was across the street. We practically owned the Cancer Ward on the third floor of Suburban Hospital. Chemo one week every month in the hospital for years.

All the boys went fucking GA GA for this petiteishly tall red head. She's got the smallest hands of any woman I'd ever met with gracefully long fingers to accent the porcelain dollish quality of her being. In the way most women are in their 20s she was standoffish. I assume from being burned and simply jealous women because she is so beautiful. She was not one to prowl the streets at night for meaty bits and pieces but when she found the man candy to mold her dreamboat come to life it twas an adventure leading up to pulsating blood, a little push and a new life that changed the game from "party on Wayne!" to "this is what you asked for, Garth."

We spent hours upon hours under the Crestwood stars contemplating what was to unfold. "It's only life." is her mantra I carry into each conquel of my heart. Even today as I walk through the central nervous system diseases I have I think to myself, "It's Only Life."

Whenever I found myself in the most precarious situations I heard her in the back of my head... Homeless, brain surgeries, heartbreaks would eventually turn into, "it's only life." don't take it so seriously... We were friends for at least 9 years so there's so Much history and so many Mysteries because I can't remember all the magic she brought into my life and made me realize the things that were causing me strife.

She made.me aware how mother used her cancer like a well-honed katana to Keep Us close. To always say, "I love you" whenever you leave the house. But it was very tiring trying to take care of a woman that didn't want my help and I didn't realize how she was being treated. The battered woman continued confused and not wanting to harm the man of the house.

She kept her biggest opinions to herself, like Andy and I weren't a good couple. If he had just been honest and told me we were open and I would have had more fun dancing with everyone. I wish I could remember all of our conversations he kept in my diary before she had her baby so that I could remember the other one having a life plan on you versus you planning on life.

Having had brain surgery I took it too seriously. I was waiting to start school. A freshman with one goal of learning Russian and letting life unfold before me as being attached to anything was problematic. Both products of divorce and the 2nd of 3 (on weekends I was 3rd of 4 but for the most part I was 2nd). Abandoned by our fathers we found very little use for boys in our click until Andy. It's always a shame when your best friends don't tell you the truth until it's over. Then it all makes sense. .

We fed on ghosts, goblins and ghouls; discussing **"Jayne Eyre"** and **"Heathcliff"**, of Byron and Shelly's absinthe binges; of the latest and greatest from Anne Rice. She loved to read romances and I love to read horror. She's the one that taught me about **Anais Nin** (this book is a tribute to **Little Birds** as well as **Anne Frank's Diary** and a continuation of **Forever** by Judy Blume. The main character's name is **Catherine** too) a virgin I awaited to be turned until I was almost 20. We listened to **"Shakespeare's Sister"** and **"Joy Division."**

Sparks was our haunt and **The Connection** (the gay bar) on occasion. We weren't sexually attracted to each other but I developed a fondness for her more than my own sisters and they were so jealous. One of the last conversations I had with my older half sister she'd told me how she'd seen "that woman" in the line at the grocery store after poisoning my mind with her infection to hate her for.loving me. She had a best friend since she was 4 but I couldn't have a friend because that cunt is a jealous whore. With the fervent reaction of my sister's demeanor I smiled inside so happy. I wanted to ask if she'd gotten her number.

Melissa remembered the exchange as Facebook reunited us again.

We were separable inseparates of a whole idea at times. It was Melissa that fueled this virgin's mind of what love was supposed to be. Teaching me the ways of Anäis Nîn and softened seduction refined. She is the real deal, genteel and kind. I was much more harsh in my younger years, always confused and indecisive, unable to maintain the many manifestations of my soul as well as comprehensive thoughts I could not control. More to the point she was one of the reasons I quit allowing my family to control me. Reclusive and outgoing I was curious about questions she seemed to have the answers for that others just *couldn't*. Supernatural too.

Listening to her kittenish voice the other day that will never reveal her age she finally got back on Facebook after 5 years. Her birthday is so deeply ingrained in my mind I wished her one and finally the smile only she can imbibe. I keep a photo of her on my fridge.

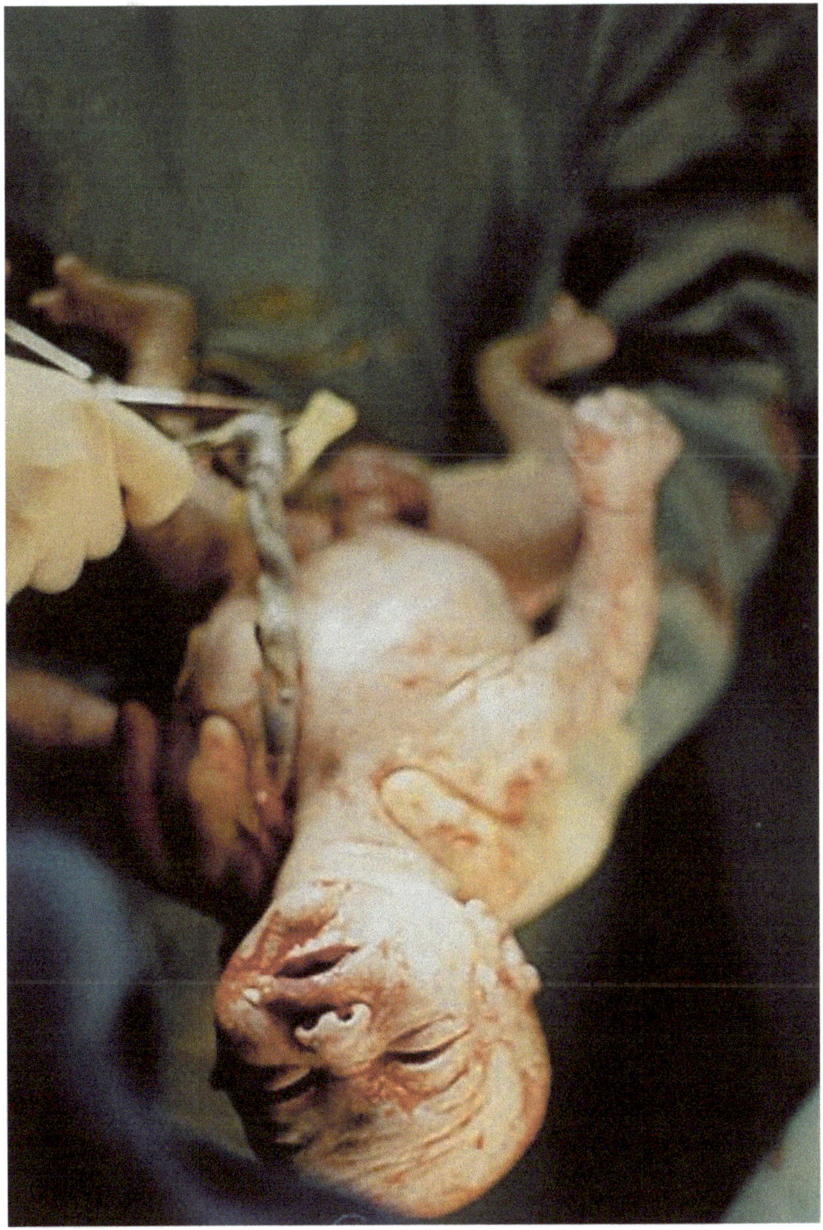

I was very lost without her but allowed myself to be swayed by my "sister's" ideals after my mother died. Going away from her

when she needed me the most after Colin was born. So this is my worst betrayal. I have this one regret that I listen to someone who **NEVER** had my best interests at heart.

We went on two cruises in the Caribbean. I've literally been to **"Hell"** and back with her.

But when she ran oft with that boy on New Year's Eve and came back knocked up, that was a game changer. It was no longer us but a baby too and I had no say so. I felt betrayed. Here was our tight friendship and when he popped out it was the most powerful moments of my life.

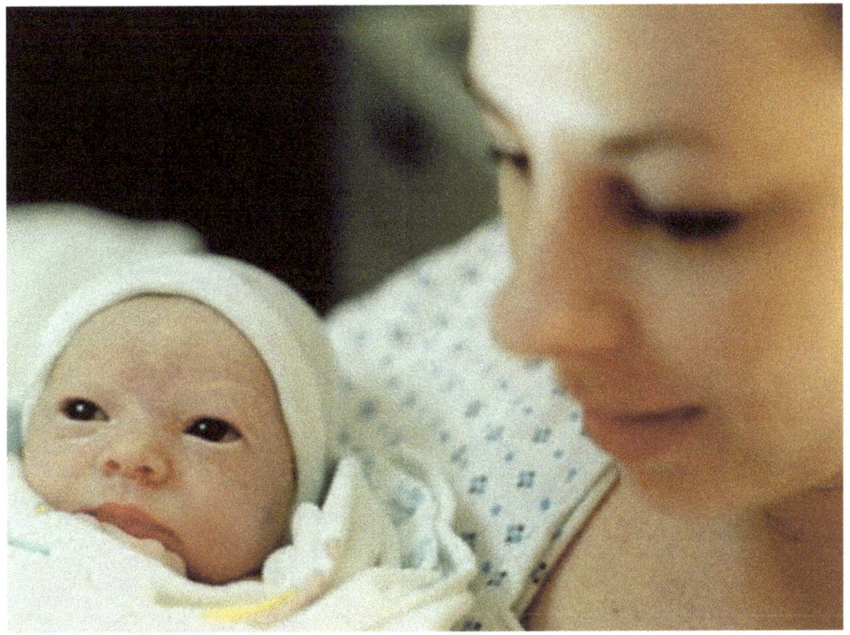

Being a labor and delivery nurse she called me when there was no question about him popping out and it seemed like I showed up just in time to cut the cord. I got a gush of blood on my sweatshirt. Such a contrast to my own delivery.

If anyone is ever lucky enough to have a friend, one friend, I wish you could all have Melissa but I can't really find the words to express the depth of 1/10th of the love and we've had the ticklish delight in sharing the fairies at night drinking wine coolers. It

Now a midwife, she'd talk about being one as well, and she didn't really get my revolution and still stays more to herself than attached to a computer. She smirked and giggled when I told her I wrote erotica. I have yet to divulge, that I know of, I hit #25 on **Amazon's "Art and Photography"** section a way back, that I am so well known for that an admiral told me every port he went to, people were talking about my book but I couldn't understand why I wasn't making money. All this 0 fame to what end?

HANDY DANDY ANDY

Is the prick to my rose.

These are two different memories. The first one I wrote a long time ago. This second one I wrote for this book.

Being a naturally born "fag hag" (used to be special not what it means today) took off the pressure. Moving through rites of passage I grew into a full woman almost 21 I met the one that I knew would be deflowering me. For he had been the one to teach my chemistry at 16.

Slowly courting six weeks the parents and places and things one must do when you think that person's in your life is a solid one to you. Seeing us play t-ball together we'd known one another for so long. Slowly we started playing with one another already in college.

We were both inexperienced lovers. Virgins to one another all that mushy stuff. I wanted someone to wake up to the next day and feel like they were going to be there each day. Who wasn't going to just run off and leave me today but someone who wanted to stay. I chose well because he's always been there for me. He's the only consistent in my life when everyone else fails me

We went to the **Hawley Cooke** on Bardstown road to read up on the subject. I found something interesting about female ejaculation.

Slowly experimenting for a few weeks getting to know each other. I had him do what they said to do which was to insert your fingers into the vagina and find the ridges and rub, rub, rub.

He rubbed and rubbed and rubbed some more.

Not experienced enough to munch on the carpet floor. It wasn't working nothing happened, we gave up because by that point I was down to fuck. He got on top of me and we made love too shy to rub on my clit in front of him. It took a second before his ass fell out of my and it was all warm. "Did you come on me ALREADY?"

He answered, "no."

Back in again and a repeat of warm wetness seeping down. my exclaiming squeals that it worked. Do it again! I was learning how my body really worked. He started pumping again. It was so hot that he lost his wad as the warmth hit his balls.

When we were growing up we are both Autistic or on the Spectrum or whatever when you have to have differences of kids opinions. We met playing t-ball with our photographs with him to my right and I was to the left. I'm both being what we are to one another.

Again up in the balcony when we were sixteen and trying to stay away from a world that wouldn't accept us for quite a hot minute. He would explain chemistry to me so it would make sense when I can always understand or get the individual attention I needed.

My chemistry teacher, Ted Bickel, will always be my favorite teacher because he went to school with my dad and he knew what a prick he was so when he threw me out he understood what was going on more than I did myself.

He had little interest in me and was so late as a teacher to a grieving child. He let me sit in the back room and cry my eyes out and come and give me a hug and tell me it was going to be all right when he knew it wasn't.

He knew what that man was capable of because he went to Centre with him.

But then our school started to split apart and we didn't get to see each other anymore. After graduation I asked him out to see a movie. Something like Parenthood and then we went home and I never heard from him again.

2 years later I was walking into the quad at the **University of Louisville** and I saw this huge grin staring at me and this amazing meat of a beautiful man standing in front of me and I went, "Oh my God!!! Hi Andy!" I was trying to diversify my life. Only the diversity wasn't wanting to be a part of me and there's nothing I can do about that but happenstance was there she went and here was right there.

That was back in the day of, "oh yeah, shucks. We just started college and we don't have any bucks." I was already over what life had to offer me but all of a sudden there was Life opening out in front of me. So ever so slowly we savored the first six weeks we spent together without having sex.

Can you imagine that now? A six-week courtship that would be unheard of unless you're living underneath somebody's glove. Christianity it's so goddamn oppressive that it kills almost everything that is living. I finally got ahold of my soul which I lost into a deep dark hole I could not dig myself out of as the abyss kept calling, "come sink with me my miss!"

We took many days learning to love each other in different ways, seeing each other from different angles, learning from each other's gaze when there's nothing else that mattered other than what was in front of your face or in between our legs.

He ended up getting mono and his mother didn't want me to kiss him after I already had it as well. I mean it's the goddamn kissing disease can't you tell?

Then we started hanging out more and more. His dormitory was such a bore. Threkstun Hall was full of boys and all they did was make a bunch of noise. Clamoring, yammering stammering and full of cum I grossed out almost all but 1.

I'd walk down the hall and rip a big fart, everyone wondering if it was a shart. I'm just like any man I piss and shit and breathe and tan. I don't know why you think we're princesses when you know what you're like, yourself.

But we learned that we did not like the dormitory accommodations so he moved in with me and my libations. His parents were being such dicks they wouldn't pay for his rent. "keep yourself in college. Don't get a job just garner knowledge." So the bill I footed.

Andy's handy dandy fingers are the reason you're reading this because it wasn't just that he was my first lover I wanted to be able to spend the night with no other. I wanted to know I was going to spend the next night with my boyfriend. And the night after that we would keep looking over never losing our sight for each other.

My first love had to be a virgin, like me, so we could feel each other being first to love one another. I can be there in that apartment in a flash and in a second feeling his hands just caressing my shoulders, lovingly fondling my breasts as they laid upon his chest. I love him so very deeply but I didn't love life completely.

I didn't think life was worth living because I didn't feel worthy of giving myself or anything that was inside me because it was screaming to be free. What I didn't know was how to express myself back then and had I known now what I didn't then I probably would have never been so down in the dumps but who needs friends when they are all chumps?

I tried to take my pain away in one Fell Swoop but it didn't stop. Naturally paramedics found me and had I only mixed the 88 muscle relaxers with beta blockers that I took you wouldn't be reading this or any of my books.

Andy never left my side except to go to his classes after I chose to die. He wanted to make sure that he knew I was there for all of that my soul was bare.

Had he only been honest a long time ago that I could go get a POA on the side I might not be on the outside of a tank looking at you as I think what I think and how I do what I do.

Andy always enjoyed the classes that I took because he never wanted to leave my side. I enjoyed being over at **Speed School** because that's what gave me the tools to find the world that wasn't so oppressive as Louisville Kentucky was in the 90s.

Andy, my first love, I will always love you and cherish the friendship that we have and do what we still do. Thanks for being the boy holding this balloon before all the air grows stale so that it no longer floats. That's what my mother used to say. "Andy's holds you like a balloon as you bounce everywhere." I'll always cherish you for so many reasons and I can't put it all in this book. Thank you for standing by my side when all I ever wanted to do was die. Thank you for making me feel loved and cherished all my life. I can't say that about any other man I know.

SUPERMAN

I had just started writing regularly when I started dating Superman. He was super. He was a Brazilian brought in from the wild to be raised in captivity by whiteys. He was the first steady cock I got after the break up with my lady love.

Being from the South there was this antebellum theme that runs deep the morrow of Southern Belle's hearts and that's gaining the love interest of a man of color. God was his cock so big and thick. I loved fucking it. Until…

Things were rolling along nicely. He started showing signs of wear and tear but when he started mentioning how the "mothership" was coming for us I started wigging a little bit. Not really knowing how to end it I just kept swimming.

My mom was dying. I didn't know WTF to do or what to think. All I knew was I had to get all the shit, all the baggage she left me with off my shoulders and she was not really in the mood for any shenanigans.

I'm bereft. I'm floating and I'm like the Titanic as the people are realizing they are definitely going to die. Mom was dying and there was nothing I could do so I tried getting her approval on everything before she died.

Superman was my cry out for help, begging my mom to stay as if to say, "Once you leave I don't know who I'm going to turn into." When I introduced this brother to my mother she was not amused. It was the nail in the coffin and I couldn't see him anymore after they met because mommy didn't approve.

She loved to tell me "There's this gray area in your thinking." which once we found out about my cyst it just goes to show you that an ongoing TBI does not bode well on a girl's ego.

I brought a black boy into her racist ideals and hoped since she was dying I could somehow change her but that was not the case. It just pissed her off. She never said anything but when she met him she didn't have to say anything, she just shook her head in disapproval.

Then to add fuel to the fire I kissed a girl and it was terrific. Got how it was so nice to kiss soft, supple lips over the stubbly hard and rough feel of a man. It was like kissing butter, or tasting ice cream for the first time, it was just breathtakingly divine. When I told her I kissed a girl she was livid but said nothing.

I was trying to tell her I didn't know who I was growing into being. That I wasn't sure if I was going to have an interracial child or just dyke out and be Lizzy the Lezzy, literally. But it passed and that was all it was, an infatuation.

(and when he grew up he was popped for kiddie porn :(~~~ and I thought my sister had the Corner Market on that one with her boyfriend that showed up into a little girl's bedroom with a machete. These stories are too good not to be real. ROTFLMFAO)

TARKOVSKY

These are two memories. The ladder memory is for this book.

German Cock, my second one, "accidentally" found me on Facebook.

(German Cock was the first man I'd cheated with. I flew from Moscow to Frankfurt for 10 days to be with him. We had a thing for Tarfkosky and he ran a fan site for it. Back in 96 when the Internet was whistling in. God how I loved what he did for me because he's the only lover that wouldn't let me leave because I flew all the way to meet him and he knew how difficult he was but I love him still the same.

I loved his cock because he still had his foreskin. It was very exciting licking the head making the skin roll on and off my tongue and back again. He was more experienced than I and asked to stick a finger up his bum which I did comply with. my nails were too long and without thinking bit it off and stuck it back in I was so intent on pleasing him.

He was indeed a cock I tried to walk out on and just forget he exists. Everyone should have a lover come chasing after them. **Rules of Engagement** I was learning quickly as him.)

Everyone should have a lover chase after them after a fight so bad you pack up all your shit ready to GTF out of the other's life. My second lover was one of them. I'm sure, if he could, he would tell me "I should have married you" but he stalked me on Facebook which is the next best thing. I can't see anything he does and he used to see everything I did until I couldn't see his life. But that is today... This was 1997.

I had my article on female ejaculation rolling on the "Post Feminist Playground" as well as having the honor of being the "Egotistical Site of the Week" for 6 months. But I found Michael, one of my angels, because he was doing the fan site for Tarkofsky, the Russian film director. I had found him and we were talking online. We were both framers and original content managers of the Internet and were into each other over our Internet status before there were "influences."

I went to Russia that year to meet up with my Finnish pen pal, Tumos Kilpi. Oh how did he spark my fire with his words. My mind, emblazoned, and on fire with all of his desire and my secret growing from 1996 to 97. I wanted to go to St. Petersburg and go over to Finland and fuck him like a freight train but he quit writing to me.

But the German Cock was there. My rebound. He wanted to meet me and he was the first ax murderer of my pussy that I'd met before POF was a glimmering site. I experienced more kink with GC in one week than I had in 3 years with the "love of my life."

I was bored sitting around waiting for GC to work so I went driving by myself. He was such an ass that he was looking for this place on the Rhine with all the castles. When we finally got so lost and stopped and ate brats and drank beer somewhere. I told him, "I was here the other day." and he did NOT believe me which pissed me way the fuck off. I told him how to drive home. I don't think he was used to dating a woman.

But the reason I love him and he's worth writing about is his was the first ass I stuck my finger up. With a fingernail that was way too sharp so I bit it off and tried again and that only made it worse so I had to stop. I was 24 and he was my second lover.

He had a huge penis that was uncircumcised so giving him a blow job was one of the more interesting events of my life considering all the hate on foreskins have received for years. It truly made me question why all the cocks with their helmets got cancer. For centuries. He was very confused why Americans were obsessed with institutional child abuse. As well as sanctioned murder. We didn't see eye to eye on the death penalty but now that I'm older I now question my younger self into putting credence in that institution even though some people fucking deserve it.

I loved Frankfurt. Even though it was leveled in the war it was all industrial, shiney and new. The fields outside his door looked like someone had some and manicured them overnight while in Kentucky when the fields were overgrown the grass was everywhere. In Germany you just walked out and it was perfect. Shit they were still using scythes to cut the grass at MGU.

We had many uncomfortable evenings but when I got up to leave in the middle of the night not knowing where I was going to go then him chasing me as I'm going down the stairs did things for my ego that no other lover has quite hit that bar except for Josh. Josh chased me into hell and didn't survive the Ninja Pussy.

I certainly noticed that bigger didn't mean better, just different so I left my lady love. I was pissed that Woobie would never have done that. That he just wouldn't step away from the computer.

I came home and had disgracefully cheated on my first love. I was tired of that relationship. It had grown stale and I had wanted to end it for years but I couldn't because Woobie was there for me when I tried to kill myself. He went to almost every class with me after my attempt to endure that I would be successful.

When I told him to move out he just stared at me blankly not understanding what I was saying. He never told me that he didn't care if we had been open, all I had to do was tell him and I was like... Oh. Well too late because if I've cheated on you then there's that flaw in me, like the way my father used to be.

After the Sniper I decided I was never going to be married again and if I was we were for certain going to be in an open relationship because I was not going to let some POA take him away from me nor me away from him. Josh fucked like a god and why would I want to deny any woman the pleasure of his being? Who was I to say "No... don't do that. I'll be mortally wounded like you killed me with your dick by sticking it in another woman." Who gives a fuck?

Never think that you are that god damn special to spend the rest of your life with one and only one when I'm here to tell you there's something else... your personal gratification. Sometimes the fairy tales are true until one day they aren't and you find yourself sleeping in your bed alone again when you really never anticipated the love of your life dropping dead... in your arms, nonetheless.

That's the lesson I learned from German Cock. Or a few. I will forever be thankful to him for freeing me into being who I wanted to be. Not some naïve woman thinking there was one and only one man out there for me when there are men and persons of interest. Michael was also a photographer and took this awesome photo of me that made me feel like I was so severely special.

I didn't love Frankfurt as much as I love Russia. Russia... there are some people that are math people, horse people but Rusophiles are all about Russia to the core of their beings and I was my father's "Ник Ник" from the time I was knee high to a grasshopper. At least up until the divorce. Then I became "the individual" to be blamed for fucking my father's life up.

When I tried drawing parallels that I was just as bad as my father and felt the guilt and shame of cheating and carrying on secret love affairs that were really just love affairs with myself. Exhibiting to me mirrors and pieces of myself that can and could be.

VLAD THE IMPALER

My first erotic photo shoot was with Vladimir. Had just gotten his PhD from Cornell and I met him at the gay bar and that's when I started having fun in Moscow. I did not like going to Moscow State University. He told me about how awful it was for gay people in Russia in 1996. I'm fuzzy on the details. It's been so long but they were awful like dragging him in the streets and humiliating them with these crazy things. He told me that artists were the highest ranking individuals in the hierarchy of who mattered. And he said, "this photograph you took of them is the most beautiful photograph I've ever seen." and he started to cry.

I love it when they start to cry because people never see how to take proper photograph and catch the Light back in the day.

My photos on *PurePhotography.Com* we're taking back in the day when if you didn't get the moment you didn't get the picture. Back when photography was an art form that is today it's just a big mess of whatever is there

These are some of the most beautiful photographs I've ever taken in my life.

THE PILOT

My mother had just died. I was bereft. It was a time you couldn't comprehend about the Internet. So many fucking id1ot ERRORS back then that pisses me off when I think of how the baby boomers had to FUCK Gen X and slapped us down making technology too big for our pants. I was two years away from seeing my first tablet and it took another 11 years to be offered to the general pubic. They burst our bubble...

But at this moment in time, before Facetime, Skype, or any visual way to communicate and BBCs had evolved more into forums there was a chat program known as **ICQ. ICQ** was the bomb. People were still using dial up. This was my summer. This is the summer the **"Uncontrollable Cunt"** was unleashed.

The first idea of a penis getting loose was written by Nokolai **Gogol** titled, **"The Nose."** It was written centuries ago and has been a popular theme for many a movie since but there wasn't a movie of a cunt out there, terrorizing the city. That was during the height of the Surrealist movement.

I had an inheritance so I decided to travel through Europe. I didn't have a destination, I just knew there were a few places I had to be at certain points in tyme. Meeting Kier in Amsterdam and go from there to my host mother in Italy. Meeting up with Roman in Russia at the end of July. Riding in a van driven by a guy for 24 hours was the most fear I've ever felt in my life but the longest I did it was 3 days. That was my way to get high.

I couldn't tell you how I came to know Kier. I guess the way all people that have come into my life and that was online. I was the first person to travel over the Atlantic keeping my dear demented diary up to date as I would photograph old school style. Before Instagram and seeing the world wasn't so mobile.

Somehow we hit it off online. Back then it was cyber sex and he was a pilot. I was enthralled at the idea of being his true to life girlfriend. My fantasies with him were just so rich and full of color. I told him I wasn't thin. I was a big girl. Over and over. When I saw him the first time, Monty Python's "hello big nose" was my reaction. He was... He was worse than any redneck I'd ever known... he was Australian. So many women from Oz have told me how worthless the lot of them are. I've found one or two worth the effort.

All this sexual energy was a lot to bear. We weren't acquainted in real life. I'd just felt sorry for him as Gala did for Dali when he wrapped himself up in shit and sat next to her. Kier would do strange things on layovers like wrap himself in a shower curtain and beat off.

Porn wasn't that big yet oh... that's how I met him. From my article on female ejaculation. He helped me cope with the death of my mother before as well as the empty nights after. The "I'll never get another phone call from her again" notion digging deep in my skin. He was so fucking callous he talked about how worms were right then eating my mother's skin. You shouldn't stereotype but we all do... This has been my random sampling.

We had just fucked and I made the mistake of asking him if he thought I was pretty.

"No."

That sent me in a spin that awoke something within as I cried myself to sleep back to back to his warm body. "I'll give you something you'll never forget nor get from another woman." were my last thoughts as we had made plans to spend a week together, if not longer.

His father had sailed his boat to meet us and the notion of sailing across the world in a tiny sailboat was something that was all weathered in his French step mother's skin.

I hated him. Oh how I hated him for making me feel less than when I was already at the start of a life I didn't know where to begin without my mother. Sleeping on the boat was not keeping us afloat as it wasn't my cup of tea to be fucking him on the bow with them sleeping so close.

My cunt was starving for his cock. We were like magnets always drawing one another in even though our minds kept screaming to stop. Then there was his cock. The night on the boat all I could keep thinking was, "If the boat's a rockin don't cum knocking." I squirted all over him and the best thing about being on the bow was watching my juice go down the drain hole. This was my first act into public sex.

I wanted my privacy even though Kier wanted to stay on the boat since he was so broke. He had to do some crazy things to make this happen. Flying with other companies while there was unrest in Indonesia which was his company's home base.

Museum, fuck, sex museum, "I need a nap" but we'd fuck instead. Our third night together I was so chafed. I didn't know about lube or if I did we weren't using it. We had to be using it because he would cyber me how he wanted to be fucked up the ass. I kept that vibrator alive for a few years. I was positive I was all washed out and we'd stop and we'd start.

My resentment grew but then he did what he did to me that I knew he'd

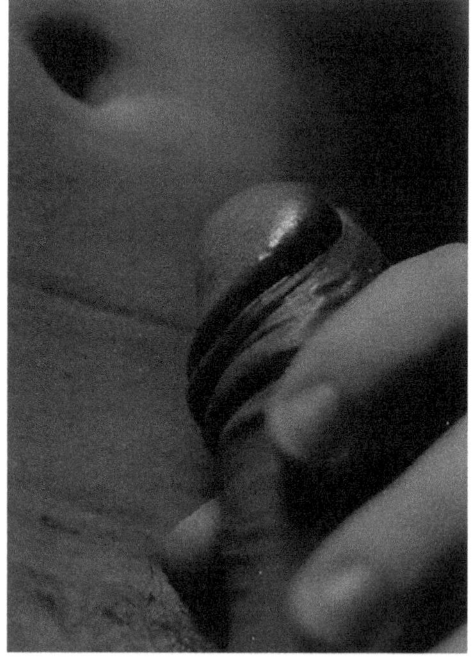

never see again and I would continue fucking like a porn star now. I'd finally gotten something I'd wished for, a guy wanting to be fucked up his ass. What a wish. He perverted my mind so very deeply grooming me to meet his desires uniquely.

I'd take out my frustration on fucking him up the ass like a titan did I feel myself wiggling to get underneath him still. With one foot on the bed and the other one next to his butt I did my best to keep it held deep within. Did I feel the gloriest of glories the vibrating cock tickling me deep inside my own cock's mind?

He had picked my fat ass up, we were the same height but I was 50 pounds heavier, and was fucking me like in a triangle motion and HOLY SHIT I couldn't believe how much I'd just come I'd lost all my wits.

We were laying there completely spent staring into each other's eyes. At least there were no lies. It was just for that one moment in tyme that we'd spend together. Him introducing me into my full blown manhood, masculinity understood and what were some of my truer perversions beginning to cook. We were laying there as two heaps and all of a sudden I started feeling something dripping on my brow and thought the pipes had sprung a leak or the rain or the... holy shit it was girl jizz dripping down from the vaulted ceiling. We were both like, "WOW?!?!?!?!?!?!!!!" (Stinky loved this story. It made him laugh especially when it was live and not part of a photograph.)

Something then awoke in me somehow. The reason I never wanted to have sex as a teen, deep seeted emotions I'd keep to myself that ran so intimately deep, so serene. I don't know if I'd have been as receptive if we weren't forced together by each other's tits, back to back. I laughed and started to howl the deliciousness of it all....

Then we went to the Red Light District hand in hand and I could tell they were trafficked sex workers from Russia and my friend Roman's voice in my ear how a friend did a gig in Turkey last year. She then came back with hollow eyes and as I looked from behind their glassed in walls through their eyes me a lady of leisure and them of circumstance. It took me years and years to understand that was not so much true, the twins were famous there and free to do what they did.

On Dasher and Dancer did we further prance here. On to a live sex show but wouldn't you know the fucking we were doing was 10,000x more extreme. We watched the scene play out and there was hardly any sex to the act he was just mostly a pole. You were supposed to leave after an hour but if you stayed you'd watch it all play out again and again. I wondered how many hours they could come and go but it was an hour and 15 then we'd leave the show. She undulated against his body in succinct choreography. I was so deeply bummed. I was expecting to see something like what we were doing, not this froofy drool.

He took me to a movie oh that was first, after the "Cannabis Cup's" 2 winner cup. "Northern Lights #5 and Haze. First we went to this theater for a bit but I didn't like it. Then I couldn't believe being higher than I'd ever been out of my mind watching a dog's dick trying to fuck a woman from behind. The men handling the dog's dick much too rough as there was blood dripping down so much god damn disgust. Then this dick coming to sit right next to me and I looked at Kier screaming GET THE FUCK AWAY FROM ME in my eyes. As he was whipping it out we ran out quickly.

We finally went to one of his friends for a quick jaunt. A place called Utrecht where we didn't fuck. Kier wanted to stay a day or two longer but I wasn't having it I was outie and he decided to stay with me his cock not knowing what the fuck was going on with it.

I loved all the museums, especially Van Gogh, but the strangest of all was about sex, don't you know? There were things there of which I could never dream. Pulps being a big part of the show. Having worked in the "Rare Books Room" at U of L I wasn't so impressed by the pulp in the cell.

There were a few photos but so much exotic stuff from China and the Arabian nights to delight ya. I wish I could have photographed but you couldn't even sneak attack like you can this day. Then we went back and fucked. That's all about the pilot.

At the end of our journey I gave him a $200 tip hoping he felt like a Giglio there for my simple entertainment.

Русалка (Mermaid)

Андрей

как я люблю яму. On так красивая и я не МОГУ., Он похоже как Стар из 50 чёрный и белый кино

Как он славят Дайвер на на море. Может Олимпик

У него есть киас близко моя подружка Людмила кем продавать косметики её была университет как бит химико инженер она так красива её есть рыжий волосы играла гитара и позже пой как птица. Её есть много друзей с кем родители на Сибирь точка И я как я тоже наши подружка. Как я сестра.

Людмила учить меня русском языке правда потому что мы рассказывали каждый день об жизнь.

Андрей работал ему и рассказывали с ним много раз. И мой второй раз там я не узнала что он нравится Мне очень много.

Он спрашивал мне если я познакомились ему и конечно я сказала да потому что я чувствовала как я не красавица но сказал мой первый очень красивая комплимент.

Когда мы заниматься любовь Он сказал что я похожа как русалка я хотела плакала потому что он так романтик.

Он слова на море Сочи и его есть так красивая обжигать кожу. Когда он Ешь меня я просто то не могу потому что у него есть очень маленький член.

Когда человек не есть очень большой член они есть как рыба надо вода.

Я могу спред когда я хочу потому что я могу делать сама ножки. Так я учила меня как как спирт когда я хочу и я спорт очень много дала его.

Он сказал я попозже как русалка как я была как "маленький русалка." У меня есть очень много вода на пизда. Падалица так много Силаева потому что я чувствовала он бедный потому что у него есть как маленький член. он абсолютно хуёва.

Когда мы были с Роман Я спрашивала ему если он хотел жить со мной на США и он сказал Нет. после ужасный Маркет на Россия 1998. Вот это абсолютно пиздец. моя сестра не понимала ничего. очень много бедных люди с кем не есть 1/3, наши деньги и это ужасный.

Когда я придумала об его я чувствую как русалка ещё с кем есть ножки.

он писал мне не один раз и он спрашивал мне, "как у тебя дела?"

У меня нет сердца скажи ничего потому что я скучала ему как я хотела ему.

ANDREI

When I was done I went back up kissing him but not with the careful ease I had earlier I wanted to feel him inside of me... My lips met his and they were so soft and wet. I kissed on him a while longer and moved my hips over his. He murmured gently from the pleasure of the moment, not so worried about what was to come but what he was experiencing at that moment.

I spun my legs and put him inside me. His face was still and then he moaned that way... the way the way we all should moan when we enter someone else that way. I moaned myself as well.

He looked at me and told me, "ты похожа Как русалка"

My heart skipped a beat. Nobody had ever said anything so romantic to me in my life. I looked like a mermaid! With my hair down covering our faces in a shadow of our own Delight. He was so beautiful and tan and hairless.

I love to watch him walk. The Swagger in his hips from being that perfect height and moving through life as an adventure every day.

I moved my hips back and forth so rhythmically just feeling him rub up against my g-spot. My face grew hot and I had to have him come out of me so I could come. It doesn't take a lot for me.

I put him back inside of me and started this way again. He started moving his hips as well and I came again. He put his hands on my ass and started to move it with my movements like a cowgirl moving his hips up and down. I went crazy and came again all wet and juicy like biting into an over ripened peach.

Then he had me lay on my back and he entered me missionary. My muscles tightened against his cock and he let out a deep, breathy moan. Resistance training ;) We went on this way his lips so close to mine. Me pushing on him. Silent and not so silent screams of pleasure. I bit on his chest.

I wrapped my legs around him. We fit so perfectly together. That as he was going in and out of me I started to shudder like a lady bug on its back. This went on for so long that it hurt and felt so good that I started to cry.

HE stopped when I pushed him out. And when he started again it was as if he was going in and out to a march playing silently in his own head. I cried out each time his cock hit my g-spot just a little. Each time when I thought he was about to finish and he was breathing as if he would he would stop for a while and regain his composure and start again.

I was going mad.

I'd never felt or experienced those sensations with anybody else. I suppose this is also the difference between making love and fucking. I used to rather enjoy fucking but now that I know the difference I think I like making love a lot better.

Edited 2021. I tried to say this in Russian but I lack the sophistication with my rudimentary Russian.

Andre had the smallest dick I've ever seen but he ate pussy like a champ. I still managed to come with a little dick the size of my pinky because I am not good.

I meant Andre in the Metro the year before while he was working selling CDs and my girlfriend was working next to him and I would always stop and talk to her.

When I went back in 1997 I was so excited to see that they were both there and what's the prize was for Andre and how beautiful he was. He looks like he stepped out of a 1950s Russian movie wearing bikini briefs burnt by the Sun from Sochi. He was ripping his boss off by buying CDs cheaper somewhere else and selling them which was very smart. When you have no money you have to think how to get out of the box.

I wasn't a small girl and I couldn't believe he was attracted to me because the self-hatred and deprecation that was taught to me by my father and mother shook me like a rag doll. Until I looked at my son and thought he was the most beautiful thing I've ever seen on Earth and then realized he was My Mini-Me.

I miss Andre. I wish I knew his last name but I miss Ludmila more. I can't find her on Facebook but this was definitely one of the hottest times because most Russian men didn't find American women attractive.

He wasn't a one-off. I asked him to go back to the United States with me so I could at least save one person and bring another voter into a "free" country. Or at least four year than Russia and much cleaner than the Russia of the late 90s.

I don't think I would enjoy it as much seeing everything so perfect without alcoholics strewn across the street going down to Red Square.

I truly learned myself when I was in Moscow because it was the first big city I chose to live in. As far the fuck away from my family so I could concentrate on me me and me after I tried to kill myself and nobody was there for me.

This was when one of my BFFs, Matt, dubbed me a "stud."

VENICE

In Venice they don't let the men into the hotels. I couldn't understand why until I finally left. Up and down up and down in and out of the canals you'll get lost without a map and keep having to double back if you're not careful.

So much romance in the air that I will always say, "Venice is for Lovers." (even thought the canals in California are a little sweeter they sure as fuck aren't neater). Alas I was loverless but feeling such a restlessness that the eye of the Italian guy I'd caught earlier was obnoxious and ever present. He was fixing the building outside.

I'd go draw and come back, a museum then a rest. I did my best to own my bliss. I kept going deeper and deeper, staying there 7 days alone with fewer to comfort me over the phone. The pilot was supposed to be keeping me company but that wasn't the case.

After being plowed open so much that it hurt to walk from chafing in Spain I had rested up and was on the prowl. But there was that worker watching me intently biding for my attention yet again and I wasn't going to waste my time with him.

By the 4th day it was too much as I craved some Italian cock to touch and finally said I would meet him outside at a certain time. We duck around the canals, not too soft nor too loud. I lift my skirt up to let him slip it in. I wonder where the "Italian Stallions" were kept because this one wasn't a bet because he was less than average at best.

I pulled one of my sneak attacks with a squirt of hot jizz but he didn't know WTF had just happened or what it just meant happens as it did.

In my bastard Italian, "Scuzzi" was practically the only word I did you know. He was not prepared for what I did in the little lair that wasn't hidden enough but nestled inside. If someone walked by us we'd surely have been seen and that was part of the fun in this scene.

He starts back at it attempting to insert his rocket but I quickly push him out to come again and he thought I was pissing all over him. He got three tickles and a squirt and I got by just barely being hurt that he didn't want to buy me an ice cream. It wasn't until much later after thinking about it he was probably married and did this often and I feel sorry for his wife because it's not a life if you lie. But I think it's just one of the things they let go.

So I always tell my men my cunt doesn't belong to them. It's on lease with the option to buy and if I'm down with someone else just know I'll be home to daddy lickidey split if he's waiting for it.

The next night was not as fun as the atmosphere was spoiled by his bitter mood over some thing else inside his idiotic mind. I bent over again, taking it like a man, as only a woman can. Again he starts to make me cum and he gets tore up as I push him out.

When he puts himself back inside me something is different, alarming and as I look up after my next squirt I realized he removed the condom.

Telling him he had to put it back on or I was off he got angry with a scoff and I huffed and I puffed and I blew him as far away until I decided to write about him today. I never wondered "If" because I didn't like the size of his cock nor his attitude, what a mockery of the hierarchy.

So ladies even if you're in the middle of it and he wants his condom off QUIT because your life isn't worth being late to visit your grave. You don't need to feel raped and guilted as you choose to love your body more than ever loving another man.

Have your fucking dignity intact instead.

WHIP IT GOOD

I never understood just how much pain I could endure until I went to Prague. I got there on a lam because I wasn't sure where I was going to go. When I was traveling I didn't know where I was going to stay, I just knew where I wanted to be. I missed my plane because I went to the Louver that day so I got a late night dormitory room.

I shared the bathroom with uptight British fuck who told me that he didn't have a wife anymore but he had four kids. And I was naive enough to believe him.

I don't know how we got to the point where our clothes were off, or at least mine oh, and he started spanking me with his belt. It started to become too painful. I was thinking we were going to be more playful.

It got so bad that I started to scream for him to stop and he wouldn't.

I wasn't quite sure if that was a type of rape or not all I know is that I wasn't asking to be beat that hard or long because I asked him to stop.

My days in Prague were beautiful. Every day was filled with an adventure and there was a girl whose shoe fell apart and I took the time to fix it.

He was in the Metro and his suitcase got stolen. I was just like, "go figure. You get out of life what you put into it." secretly I was laughing.

I spent $50 eating at a Russian restaurant with food that wasn't so great but Russian Cuisine isn't known to be the finest.

I drink a Pilsner Urquell overlooking the Vltava River as the water falls, lending Dewey drops into the night. I'm leaving the air with a glowing mist.

Walking in St Petersburg is like walking on a wedding cake but walking through Prague is like walking into a fairy tale. You can see where so many people are so inspired by so much Beauty. It was overwhelming at times so I would have to go back to the dorm just to decompress from all the unique Gothic Beauty that had been such a part of my life as it filtered into our society.

I extended my stay to meet Jean Saudek as he was signing his photographs. It was overwhelming. He asked me where I was from. "Kentucky! Kentucky! Kentucky! I was in Kentucky in 1969." (I have since discovered that he goes to the **St. James Art Fair** quite regularly from Kim Bell.)

"Please let me be your assistant."

"I can't. I mean look at these bitches sitting next to me and they can't even speak English." But I wasn't one he wanted to fuck.

The mirror did not go all the way down so I could not see just how badly that fucker beat me. When I said `` shut up to Moscow 10 days later my host mother looked at my back and was aghast. "Katya, where did you get these marks from?"

I didn't even know what to say to her because I was so ashamed. Ashamed to tell anybody what had happened to me because I asked him to do it well. We got to the point where we were comfortable enough to let him do that to me.

That's when I discovered just how high of a tolerance for pain that I have because he beat me pretty bad to leave that many marks on me.

I never let a man ever touch me like that again except for **Whip It Good** and that was out of love not hate. That man hated women and took it out on me. I don't know how I get to be that lucky.

I guess it's because of the way I look.

JACINTA

Sunday January 9, 1999

The lights flashed continually assaulting those that just sat and watched. Jacinta asked me to come out with her last night to Club Salsa. I danced, I boogied, I did Tae Bo on the dance floor and everyone started laughing. I got tired. I sat down and I watched other people as they danced lasciviously.

I watched all the different couples but there was one that almost made my heart stop. I watched as they moved together with intimate knowledge of one another's body. She moved her slender hips with just a little more sway than all the other beauties. Her legs were wrapped around his and he controlled her every movement.

His hips betrayed what kind of lover he was. He was a big man towering over most of the men in the room. His skin as smooth as a baby's butt and his hair dark. He still had a boyish quality about him as well a streak of meanness that translated into a sort of frivolous attitude as he commanded her body to move in sync with his own.

She reached up and caressed his cheek so lovingly. They kissed and giggled and delighted in themselves and the world around them just seemed to melt away. The lights, the sound, the people were all incidental as their expressive bodies demonstrated how they felt about one another. The tempo changed and he moved her body around him much faster and his hips swayed in mock carnal delight.

I found myself filled with the vapors and somehow feeling like I had been witness to something that was forbidden. I looked back at Carolyn in her shiny top and tight pants and we both laughed as I fanned myself. I wished I had my camera... but I know they will be there again next week.

ZACK

I woke up from my dream to answer a query from Zack. He asked me to step into the kitchen from a wonderful dream which left me only with good feelings. For some reason Zack's query startled me... like when my father used to wake me up and yell at me. He has a simple question about the gravy... nothing that was to cause such apprehension. Strangely, I thought that no one ever wanted to harm me.The conversation we had last night stirred up many feelings I had not shared with anyone in a while.

Feelings I kept deep inside of me. Traumatic things that I've felt the world could see tattooed on my head. Zack talked about a lot of things as well. What she was most jealous of was the consciousness he carried not to have the desire to take his own life. To have never have felt so bad as to even attempt suicide although I know everyone still thinks about it.

He told me the three things that occupies people's mind the most are sex, food and death. I believe it.

As we were falling asleep I said "I'm glad you are my best friend. I love you so much." So many things flashed in my mind as I said this. How he stuck up for me when they censored (*CatherineClay. Com/censor*) photos down. How he looked when he was 18 and we were in Russian together our first semester. How he used to walk around the hall in school. The way his art flowed together to make a congruent body of work. So many shared memories that enriched their relationship to deeper levels. How we supported one another through the best and worst of times. Even some of the more mundane times.

I knew in her heart that I am closer to him then I could be with anyone. I admired his strength of character and his kind heart and loving nature... and his beautiful hatefulness, so unique and individually Zack. His humor, his wit and his sometimes bitchy nature that was so endearing to my heart. I saw him for the great man that he was instead of what he sometimes wanted me to believe what he believes . Sometimes I have to remind him, myself.

He talked about how some things were of such a personal nature... how what I went through with my mother made me appreciate things maybe other people couldn't. This is what I define as being a beautiful person. Someone that understood and feels the implication of their life as they move through it. Understanding the responsibilities of my actions and doing the best I can to not hurt anyone.

I knew I would be there for him when life started to throw him around. I would know the right things to say to make it be ok just as he simply loved on me this week after my mother died. But for now I took in his stories and delighted in the intricacies of his travels and his art. Absorbed in his imagery.

My heart felt lighter after last night. I told him how I used to live in constant fear. When I moved in with my mother I had been extremely violent. There was not a door at my mother's house that had its original jambs.

I bridled my temper and rage in order to make me a better artist. I thanked my father for one thing and one thing only and that was my overwhelming discipline. Being the daughter of a one time drill Sergeant had its advantages.

But I did not like living in fear of people. I tried to explain my extreme extroverted personality to my grandmother just the other day... that by being more extroverted people tended to leave me alone and not ask any questions I was not be comfortable with.

I felt that I was getting away from those thoughts that used to consume my mother... that my mother had inflicted upon me. I felt like I was becoming my own person.

We also discussed money and how we were raised. I told him that when I was 15 and moved in with my mother and all we had to eat were pot pies and peanut butter sandwiches where before daddy had eaten steak and lamb. I told Zack that I wouldn't trade those memories for all the money in the world because I appreciated the life I had with my mother more because it had been emotionally satisfying.

We both agreed that the most important thing in life is having rich emotional connections.

Too bad drugs came between us, more me being on Fentanyl than his drug of choice but that wasn't great either. And the Atkins diet.

LONDON CALLING

This isn't only a sex story. It demonstrates a pattern of Family Violence and calls attention to how Arab men have BS ideals of the way a woman should behave as if she were a man, excuse me has a penis.

It was 99 or Y2K.

I don't know how we MET but he found me. Most of the people that I met online wrote to me because they met me through my diary.

I don't know why I found this guy so fascinating but he wrote my name in Arabic and sent it to me and I thought that was romantic.

Apparently he had a different idea of who I was and I kept warning him how I really was and I think he made up his mind that I was somebody else. The blond bombshell with big tits.

He was a Jordanian architect and he was such a prick. He came from the old school tradition of how women should behave and how they have their own place.

If I have to pick the worst lover in the world it was this fucking pick. Next to my rapist. He took maybe 10 minutes and then asked me why I was sleeping with him and not my sister. The whole situation got too weird.

It really jaded my feelings towards Arabic men because that wasn't the only run-in that I've had with a Persian man who took me for granted.

It was so bad that we had to leave and stay in a hotel that was so expensive. My sister didn't want to go anywhere and stayed on the phone talking to her boyfriend the entire time.

We went horseback riding in Hyde Park. That was pretty cool because I was speaking Russian to the little girls that were taking care of the horses and as I was riding the little girls thought it would be funny if they could smack the horse so I could catch up.

The only good advice my sister ever gave me was, "if a horse ever gets away from you, hold on with your knees" for dear life and it's happened twice to me and I wasn't thrown.

She thought she was really funny. Especially when she said, "if I can control a thousand pound animal in between my legs I can handle a man." She had really bad taste in men.

So this guy that we were riding with asked the Russian attorney I was speaking with asked, "where is she from in Russia?"

"I'm not Russian, I'm from Kentucky."

We keep riding and then he finally asked me, "What's your name?"

"Catherine Clay."

A few more minutes go by. "Are you any kin to Martha Ann Clay?"

I'm really excited at this point, "she's my aunt I exclaimed!!!"

"She's our best friend." here was somebody in front of me who is best friends with my aunt!!!

I was so excited because of the possibility of having a job in London was making me so happy. Just a dream.

Thinking back the last time I saw my Aunt Martha Ann was when my father beat my mother into the Spitfire she was driving. It's a soft top convertible and he hit her into us and we never saw Aunt Martha again. No more Thanksgivings and no more Christmases.

I get so excited when we get off the horses and I explain to Anne, "He's best friends with Aunt Martha Ann." I'm so excited at this point because of the possibility of getting out of the hotel and having dinner.

"I'm sorry," the snot-nosed bitch ruined my little fantasy as she always did.

I had a professor named Jake Kloner who taught "Surrealism," an art history course, said, "as soon as you get the key to language you can understand every language."

So we went to the bar and more chit-chatting with the bartender. My sister loves to talk about how she was majoring in Spanish and I don't speak a lick of Spanish except, "caiete La Puta Boca."

So she was trying to impress me with her skills with a bartender and he finally asks her colloquially, "where are you from?"

Blink. Blink blink.

I finally look at him and say, "She's from Lexington and I'm from Louisville." And the spell that she was casting upon him was broken. That was the hotel bar.

Let her stay the fuck alone in the hotel.

I finally went out by myself and enjoyed myself. God damn company. I wanted to find a Gay bar but the bitch wore my last nerve.

I told her not to park her car in the back of **St James Court** and she did it anyways. It was broken into.We walked up to the top of the steps and she started hitting me and I've never wanted to throw someone down the steps as bad as I did in that moment and I had to stop myself from killing my own sister as she beat me.

They were the stone steps as there was no way she would have survived if I had just pushed her off of me but I couldn't do it. I just let her hit me for the last time.

SLAP MY BITCH UP MY FIRST PERSONAL RAPE

It was a dark and stormy night like in Rocky Horror in Louisville and I was about to do something I'd never done. I'd finally started popping down walls after my mother died writing **Tales of the Uncontrollable Cunt**. I was writing for something I'd never read about. When "Catherine" grows up from Judy Blume's book, **Forever.** I had read so many eons before. 10 years. In internet years that's millennia and I was destined to extoll the virtues of "Catherine" as she aged. "Catherine Elizabeth" entitled for being named for two queens but as I began to count recently over 20 queens its impact was far greater than my mother would quip as she brushed my fair hair as a child.

I was on the prowl as I found my first rapist. I was enjoying sneak attack squirting on Ys. Being that one girl that really can and not just from a porn he saw. Or thought I was European. Being that boy that grew into a man with her own thoughts and desires much more perverted than a Y's I do not need pornography to enhance my performance.

I'd ushered in the squirter subculture for the interent in 1997 with an article for the **Post Feminist Playground**, yet another story, because Susanna Breslin doubted its very existence to which I wrote a very popular article. (and 21 years later I've only perfected my technique.

Y's lack so much imagination because they have to use porn as inspiration. Motivation to being a person fine as who you are living in your (dinging pointing at you behind the screen) skin, the great and all powerful Oz. I certainly enjoyed making it much more than I did faking it and love to watch myself give my deceased husband head. Even though I've lost my sensation to "widow cunt" I still get off watching younger me pleasing my then living "tinker" of my own.

Out and about I ended up at THE bar of the 90s to go to all things **U of L, The Granville Inn**. I chose it over **The Tavern** for the quality of men and boy did I know how to pick one. A man with boyish charm that was more than likely gay and trying really, really hard to prove his manhood by fucking a fat girl is what I surmise.

I gave him the old faithful she's known for but was quickly tapped out and had no lubrication. (I didn't learn about that well into my 30s)

Y's were born knowing they were born to give it just like women are born knowing we have to take it. It's in our DNA. Pathways that go back for centuries. No matter how safe my son will keep his daughters from being poisoned his mother was still raped because she made a choice.

A choice to use her own body as she desired. Something else that most of my son's generation will never know of as they take comfort fucks with NSA. When girls weren't "In it to win it" for another notch on the belt. Another restless night not spent being so young.

My father had raped so much from me. Took away my right to be in my own body instead of seeing my mother minus a generation in which to shift his alcoholic frustration. My brother called me his favorite pet name for me when I told him, a "liar."

He raped my mother first when they were young, then as they aged in married bliss and then by divorcing her for having cancer then took her kids away. Sounds familiar? He raped us by thinking it was going to be so easy raising 3 children every Sunday at 5 pm on the DOT - Friday, no matter what. Military man that he is. He'd laugh about raping his clients. (I can remember when he put your father away, Foxy. He used so many racial epitaphs. One I'd learnt that day. Couldn't wait to put that "*** **** ***** drug dealing mother fucker away. Laughing with that whistle he does, wheee hee hew.)

I know I'm giving my father too much power by even mentioning him and casting dispersions his way for being the raping coke whore alcoholic pedophile he was until I was 15. He took my virginity from me when I was 10 because he took me to a gynecologist. Josh didn't think that 10 was too young because, "Girls have that done." I'd never been so admonished when he didn't realize how young 8 was and neglected to demonstrate by pointing it out to him when our son was 8.

And I told Dr. Patel the last time I saw him he said he was sorry because he knew how young that was and how it can fuck somebody up.

You see he'd taken us away from her by taking a judge through the house when she was in the hospital getting her guts sliced opened the first time from Ovarian cancer (Dr. Michael Baker was such a fucking idiot she *couldn't* *possibly* have ovarian cancer 8 years later since he removed her ovaries *already*). In all my years of being a woman and seeing Gyns don't go to a man. They don't know how we work. They really don't know how we feel.

I saw Judah Renan and made a joke about the big Jewish cock and I started laughing because that, "hasn't been my experience." Then he told me I needed a hysterectomy Before Christmas telling me I had Adenomyosis when they were just adhesions. Never test them stupid fuck that says this shit to you. Get a second opinion before you lose a holiday because some fuck hates you for laughing at him.

Momma had to rent rooms to keep the house T. tried taking from her as well as us. When I started discharging at 8, because that's what little girls can do before they start their periods, my mom quipped, "You have VD." I told a friend of mine and my friend's mother told my father.

Now did he ASK me if this was going on? No... remember I was always a "liar" and instead of asking me I was told by his secretary, Patty Abel(the only secretary that took an interest in our well being that he left my mom for), that I was going to see one of these Dr.s and asked if I wanted a man or a woman. I didn't get a chance to talk to my mom about it. He didn't trust me to tell the truth so he raped me from feeling myself as a whole person by the time I was 10. Which is why I knew how my sister felt but never told her.

I didn't understand that my mom was trying to tell me gently that my father was, like the creep in **Something About Amelia** molesting me. Amelia's dad was raping her but since T. never REALLY inserted his penis inside me I couldn't tell people he was because I didn't understand the complexities of being molested at that point in my life.

He made me sit across from him for eight years so that he could watch me thinking of my mother. He never wanted to look at his girlfriend's, he just wanted to watch me eat and when you are a prey in front of an apex predator you start to understand that icy glaze isn't just for your discomfort it's for his comfort masturbating. You start to pick up on it as you age.

He spanked the living fuck out of me and I learned he was abusing me in **Sex Crimes** as spanking is a form of molestation because "it brings blood to the vaginal area." He'd spank me so fucking hard he'd leave bruises on me but not his "baby."

I was acceptably raped by the medical community and then went for ice cream afterwards but melted in heaving sobs into my mother's massive breasts that Friday. It was a Monday, the first day of 5th grade, I was 10. I had to wait to go to my safe haven 5 days later.

I never believed my sister when she'd say, "I love you" because our father had done it to me and I had nobody to talk to about it. I cried once but was never the same again and had taken my self loathing out on her. Like most sexual assaults you put it behind you and try to go through the motions of life pretending that it never happened until you are in your 30s or 40s and realize you never had the capacity to deal with it.

That and being raped by a religious zealot that donated enough Catholic guilt to last the rest of my life when I was caught by a fanatic with her son in a closet when I was 8. We were just curious children but I kept screaming, "Please DON'T TELL MY DADDY!!! PLEASE DON'T TELL MY DADDY!!!"

I went home that night to my sister telling me how beautiful I was and how she loved me and that was when I had started the annellation myself. I hated her for loving me much like my sister hated me for loving her. Teaching myself how you could never trust women plus the sexism I was being raised with didn't help.

Raping myself. I had nobody to talk to about it.

So my first full blown rape was when I'm with Mr. Last Call for Alcohol in my apartment on **St. James Ct**. I was enjoying who I was and then I kept trying to get him to cum. He started getting frantic because he couldn't get off. I kept blaming myself because he couldn't. I was too fat and too ugly, like my father had programmed me.

I wanted this creep off of me and instead of screaming, "GET THE FUCK OFF OF ME" because I'd taken him home. I let him inside me. I'd been drinking. I was sleeping with strange men at the drop of my pants. I'd been "asking for it" but I was waiting for it to be over, for him to finally cum, slide the condom off and walk out my door.

Mr. LCFA kept going and going and I was lying like a dead fish when I'd started as a willing participant only I couldn't just stop him and escort him out the door because that's what bitches do and although I was OneOpinionatedBitch.Com I was not going to stop him. Nobody ever taught me how. Or that even if I didn't feel comfortable that I could make a guy stop at any moment and tell him to get the fuck off of me.

Part of it was because of my brain tumor you get to age with. I started the Arachnoid Cyst foundation, *acyst.org*, because, as I've discovered so many of us as children are molested and raped. We are easily led so predators know what to look for when they are on the lookout. That was also the reason for my masculine take on my own sexuality.

I waited for him to finish and cum, but "thank God, the big invisible cock" (that wrote it was OK for women to be raped because they couldn't see our tiny little cocks OR recognize that we had orgasms too) that he didn't so I didn't have to live with his spunk inside me the rest of my life too.

All kinds of shit goes through your head when you are raped. I DESERVED it for enjoying my body the way Ys or other men enjoy theirs. I DESERVED it for not going to church and being a "good girl." I DESERVED it for it being last call and I took him back to my flat.

He just got up off of me and put his clothes on and walked out the door leaving it open as I lay there, naked. My head coming off the bed watching him leave upside down saying to myself, "that wasn't rape. I wasn't just raped. Not me. Not my pussy. I asked for it. I deserved it."

I went about my day the next and went to where I could for comfort after my mother died. My grandparents. I went to church the next day. Set up taking photos of us that day. I ran into the bathroom and delivered a condom before church praying for God's forgiveness in trying to be a man on my own terms. I was 25. A woman.

I DIDN'T DESERVE IT.

101 Shades of Clay wouldn't be complete without these stories as every girl's sexual awakening starts somewhere and this is how mine began. In honor of the girl's trial that was raped by some weak slime bag that drugged a woman to get her to fuck him, otherwise she'd never look his way, is the most repugnant form of rape a woman can experience.

Brushing lint off shoulder.

In honor of all the faceless women that would just rather forget about that trauma that her body can not as it's betrayed her so when she meets someone that has been raped she is more sympathetic, even if he becomes a rapist. Even when you hear about some poor dude raped by another woman you secretly feel a joy in your heart that at least one poor bastard knows what it's like to be raped.

I salute you fucking cunts for crossing that first one off your "fucked it" list. You're NOT (emphatically pointing my finger at YOU the way my father would point his finger at me when he'd call me a LIAR) WORTHY of the self hatred, PTSD, inability to enjoy your body for you own. QUIT FEELING GUILTY YOU "DUMB CUNT." And quit calling yourself that. It serves NO PURPOSE. You're not a god damn "survivor" your a FUCKING "THRIVER".

Quit buying into the life that textbooks define us by and free your body by freeing your mind. You're never going to "GET OVER IT" you just need to "GET WITH IT." You'll never "move on" or "forget about it" because what most dingus' don't understand that every time you hear the word "rape" your ears, your skin, the sweat on your brow, and the taste in your mouth pricks up as you hear yourself as it's happening to you all over again and again. No matter how many moons have transpired there will be something that sets something off inside you much like when a gay man hears the word "fag" you need to divorce yourself from the connotation that it's something bad. It just is what it is and get with it.

Oh and that photo I snapped with my grandparents... my half sister and Stith Funeral Home raped me because they weren't going to take down a photo slideshow without my permission showcasing the photo of me fat, ugly and freshly raped to be a part of the internet, forever. I salute you, Lesli Poynter, for being the petty, jealous, insensitive creature you are.

Once you've been raped it's not something you brush off of you it grows with you, organically. Like the first time you're introduced into pleasure you don't know if it's wrong or right it just is what it is and you feel how you do. Others talk about it but don't guide you out of it.

I don't know how I do but I do what I do.

Don't think you've washed that "rape target" off your back the way we are continually raped saying that it didn't happen to us. That there are one in four other bitches feeling the way you do about yourself that they haven't or won't feel about themselves because it's not one in four it's that every woman is raped at least FOUR TIMES IN HER LIFE.

My mother was dead and it was my first birthday without her. I told Kevin but he could go home and jack off dreaming of my hot wet pussy. So the next day, my birthday, we got together and fucked like minx. I took charge of our sexualiry because I knew who I always wanted to be once I knew what living was all about.

"Did you wank it?"

"Yes I did." he admitted honestly. Because of that Honesty you can do something our relationship got kicked up a few levels rather abruptly because that night was the night I got my favorite nickname. The Ninja Pussy, HIYA! "She's got a kick."

I love the way he would convey his feelings towards me when his cock was buried deep inside of me. He was humiliated that he worked up a sweat but I loved to feel it drip as much as I lived feeling his hotter than cold wet balls slapping my ass as he'd pump into me again and again.

'You've turned me into a pot smoking sex fiend."

He was the first and last man to ever break my heart. Not the kind of heartbreak Josh did when he left me because I've always been the one to leave.

But if I like someone and I WANT to spend time with them I won't fuck them on the first date. That complicates things exponentially because you never get a true sense of what a human being is really like and what they're going to mean to you.

Even with the abrupt intimacy that the internet lends, it still doesn't beat the face to face reality and sharing of pheromones brings to its traction together forming a chemical bond unlike any other making ions and matter that didn't exist before you came together.

I love (even if I saw Kevin today) thinking about him whispering, "you've got a pussy with a kick. A **Ninja Pussy**" because I like the force a guy do you have a greater pump than a double action shotgun. When he whispered that in my ear our first encounter on my birthday in 1999 I knew I had met one of the greatest loves of my life.

Of all the lovers I've ever had he has the filthiest mouth that would say the most beautiful and vile things while he was deep inside of me. The most vile being, "you're more beautiful when my cock is inside of you." I see myself having orgasms and I can understand why he would say that.

I don't understand why there has been no other man that can articulate his own desires by turning me into a pot smoking Sex Fiend too. I wasn't HYPER sexual until I met Kevin and he opened Pandora's Box of my desires.

I'll never feel the way about anyone else the way I still feel about Kevin even after all these years. And perhaps it wasn't him as much as I enjoyed my own company while I was with him. I really like the person I was and who he allowed me to be when we were together and with his friends.

Whenever I think of your face all I can see is you dubbing me **"The Ninja Pussy." vs** being an **"Uncontrollable Cunt"** because some other dick called me "Uncontrollable" and from **Truly Tasteless Jokes** I knew I had a "Cunt" since I was 8 I just didn't get the full **Jena se qua** until I got older

NINJA PUSSY

My mother was dead and it was my first birthday without her. I told Kevin but he could go home and jack off dreaming of my hot wet pussy. So the next day, my birthday, we got together and fucked like minx. I took charge of our sexualiry because I knew who I always wanted to be once I knew what living was all about.

"Did you wank it."

"Yes I did." he admitted honestly. Because of that Honesty you can do something our relationship got kicked up a few levels rather abruptly because that night was the night I got my favorite nickname. The Ninja Pussy, HIYA! "She's got a kick."

I love the way he would convey his feelings towards me when his cock was buried deep inside of mc. Hc was humiliated that he worked up a sweat but I loved to fell it drip as much as I lived feeling his hot than cold wet balls slapping my ass as he'd pump into me again and again.

'You've turned me into a pot smoking sex fiend."

He was the first and last man to ever break my heart. Not the kind of heartbreak Josh did when he left me because I've always been the one to leave.

But if I like someone and I WANT to spend time with them I won't fuck them on the first date. That complicates things exponentially because you never get a true sense of what does human being is really like and what they're going to mean to you.

Even with the abrupt intimacy that the internet lens it still doesn't beat the face to face reality and sharing of pheromones bring to its traction together forming a chemical bond unlike any other making ions and matter that didn't exist before you came together.

I love (even if I saw Kevin today) thinking about him whispering, "you've got a pussy with a kick. A **Ninja Pussy**" because I like the force a guy do you have a greater pump than a double action shotgun. When he whispered that in my ear our first encounter on my birthday in 1999 I knew I had met one of the greatest loves of my life.

Of all the lovers I've ever had he has a filthiest mouth that would say the most beautiful and vile things while he was deep inside of me. The most vile being, "you're more beautiful when my cock is inside of you." I seen myself have orgasms and I can understand why he would say that.

I don't understand why there has been no other man that can articulate his own desires by turning me into a pot smoking Sex Fiend too. I wasn't HYPER sexual until I met Kevin and he opened Pandora's Box of my desires.

I'll never feel the way about anyone else the way I still feel about Kevin even after all these years. And perhaps it wasn't him as much as I enjoyed my own company while I was with him. I really like the person I was and who he allowed me to be when we were together and with his friends.

Whenever I think of your face all I can see is you dubbing me **"The Ninja Pussy." vs** being an **"Uncontrollable Cunt"** because some other dick called me "Uncontrollable" and from **Truly Tasteless Jokes** I knew I had a "Cunt" since I was 8 I just didn't get the full **Jena se qua** until I got older.

GOOD LOVIN'

Tuesday January 4, 1999

He touches me these days and he does it so tenderly. It's as thought we have given up any inhibitions we felt before now and started to appreciate one another more and more. I let him do things to my body he has only fantasized about.

I think that's one of the problems. I feel like men are surprised that women want them to touch them or fuck them real hard. It's as though the things men imagine are forbidden in this culture, so they keep a straight face and are pussy whipped into submission.

Which led me to think that sure he can wear the pants in this relationship but never forget who has the whip.

So... I went to visitation last night and it made me very sad. Three of his own children did not bother to come to his own funeral. I saw my father there last night and introduced him to Kevin. It was very awkward. I told him I was sorry and went to shake his hand but he went in for a hug instead. I am about the same height he is now. Funny how scared I used to be of him and think he was so large when I was a child.

The best part of last night was eating fried steak and gravy at Granny's. She is still upset about my homo-erotic photos. We had a little chat about homo-sexuality and I told her how I didn't think it was wrong. This was the way some people express their sexuality and any kind of love is not abhorrent in my eyes. Violence and hate is much more disgusting in my eyes.

She offered to buy my photographs in order to destroy them and I wouldn't let her because that would defeat the purpose and basically ruin my self- esteem. She did not agree. She bitched about how awful my brother was to her about not even bothering to thank her for her Christmas gift to him and I told her to fucking forget about that bastard. He is not worth the breath coming out of her mouth because he will remain a pathological liar until the day he dies.

I am just sick of hearing about it because there are so many better things to talk about then what people do to hurt me as an adult. I feel that as a child there was nothing I could do to protect myself and sometimes I still feel helpless.

Kevin jumped my shit about allowing other people to take advantage of me. He also told me that I shouldn't get so worked up about some of the things my friends say or do to bother me. None of them are saints and nothing they say is the gospel truth. Sometimes I forget this fact and let myself live my life through other people's eyes or even worse, through their own view of how I should behave. Being raised to be a people pleaser didn't help much.

I got this book titled Why you behave in ways that you hate and hopefully when I am through with it I can actually practice some of the things I am learning by not allowing things to bother me like I am a child.

I would love to go on and on but I am subbing today. I think I would just like to sub for academic classes from now on. I had two Russians in my Calculus class earlier so I got to practice a little. I can't help them much but absolute values are easy to remember.

My cousin Julie told me my father was really torn up about his dad dying. I wonder how he feels now knowing his brothers and sister didn't care enough to even bother coming to his funeral. I wonder if it will be an eye opening experience. I'm not going to hold my breath. I showed him I was a better person than he is by acknowledging the death of his parent when he didn't even bother to acknowledge the death of my mother to me.

TAKE MY BREATH AWAY

Thursday July 29, 1999

When he first puts himself in me... it takes my breath away and I always mutter "oh God." He looked at me last night after we left the party and asked me why when we have sex it feels different than the time before. I have no easy answer for that. I just know that every time we are intimate, it just feels different each and every time. I don't know how it can feel this way, but it does.

It's like we both forget what it's like to be in one another... and every time it feels different so it always feels new. I think part of the problem we both have with one another is that we both feel such strong, overwhelming emotions when we are together. Emotions we haven't found with other people that we get mad at the other person for making us feel this way. I know I never anticipated being overwhelmed... and I know sometimes when he comes home from work all stressed out and he tries taking it out on me that he is just frustrated because he doesn't want to admit that he is overwhelmed with emotion.

But I am the same way. I won't tell him I love him because I am scared that this will be taken away from me. I am scared that the good times will evaporate and the sex will only come once or twice a week instead of everyday.

I will be thrilled when all this moving business is over. I can't wait until we are settled and we can fall into a better routine.

Last night he was a little tipsy and he went on forever. I'm very sore today... rubber burns. And I am very empty. I love feeling this way so that he can fill me back up . I think about him most of the day, what things are going wrong, things he lets fly out of his pie hole that bear no consequence to him but enrage me just the same.

Today I am going to think about last night. Good God it was so passionate and so much better than before, but that always seems to be the case. I knew on my birthday that this could be interesting because I have never seen a man with such a short refractory period... He says that it confuses him too. I don't think he knows where the stamina comes from. At this point I just don't give a shit. I like having at least three orgasms in one hour. I can live with that. And when my body is so responsive to the things he does to please me it furthers his willingness to please me more.

I love this time in my life... I hate moving, but I love the change. When I think about how I wanted to die I get a little sad and am grateful that I didn't because I never knew such passion could exist between two people. I know that I feel like a better person these days... more forgiving, more loving, just more everything.

I wish my good mood could rub off on people but I am finding that that idea is a near impossibility. Oh well, I think it's enough that I feel so much on my own.

He said something last night that disturbed me... like there is going to be something else that might come along and make this life, these sensations just disappear. Like there is some foreboding looming in the background. I am personally sick of living my life in such a manner. I lived that way when mom was alive. Damian came over the day before and told me all the shit going on in his life and I was thankful for a change that my life has been peaceful. I think I deserve it.

I wrote a letter to my dad telling him I would forgive him if he would do what he said he would and pay for my college education. I don't know what is wrong with me and why I get these notions that for some reason my father still cares about me somewhere in his heart. My brother then ridiculed me for it because he felt threatened. I am glad to know his position isn't so secure with my father.

But I also know in that little exhibit of anger that he still ridicules me himself, and that will never change no matter what kind of wonderful person I am. I hurt my father by reacting to his abuse in a manner as equally offensive as his abuse. He ruined my childhood with his selfish ways(and NOW I know he's a Coke whore)... and my reaction to his abuse was excessive but what alternative did I have?

He refuses to admit he did anything wrong to warrant such strong emotions and now I just pity him. I thought I could love him once again, but I have decided that he is better off in a past that can never be resolved. The gordian knot he now is because I've untied myself from the pretzel he turned me into. My life still continues and no matter how hard he tries to convince me that I am worthless myself, I find other people, good people that live their lives responsibly, love and care about me.

I can no longer worry about what he can and can not do for me because he is so far removed from my life, and I think I am much happier that way. I don't have to listen to him bitch or tell me how to live my life. I hear some people complain about their own fathers and I smile to myself because I know I don't have to deal with that shit.

However there is a side that continues to grieve. That part I can not let go so easily. The part that didn't get a car for her 16th birthday (not like he would have gotten me a car anyways); the part that didn't get to enjoy a cocktail for the first time when she was 21 with her daddy; the part that knows he will never be there when I walk down the aisle or kiss my children on their newborn heads. These things mean something to me... which is why I have been so careful about the relationships I have had with men. I didn't care to please myself, sexually, and be a slut. I loved that part of myself when I didn't have to listen to a man bitch and complain about his day at the office. But on the other side I know that I will choose a man that will be a daddy to his little girls. Who will teach them how to drive, who will kiss their fears away and who will love their mother until the day she dies.

I deserve that kind of man and nothing less. (and I had that in Josh in so many ways until he faltered.)

So... when Kevin is on top of me, pleasing me in his very special way, this kind of life where I am loved so deeply is the only answer to his question of why it's so good between us. Because he **understands** what it means to lose a parent, and he **understands** how important life means **today** because there is always something in the background... looming to take it all away.

I can't imagine feeling this way for anyone else (I still haven't. I am sorry I was a cunt to you the most, Kevvy Joe. I guess that's because I loved you so much until the day you told me you didn't because daddy), and I am not sure I even want to. Life is too short and I think I have a great man, someone who is as great to me as I am to myself... even if it's just all in my mind.

He talks dirty to me as he slides it in and out. He tells me how he feels when he is deep inside of me and how much he loves my pussy. It makes me use every muscle in my body to push on him harder, with as much force as I can muster. He gets harder and faster in me when I push and that forces my G-spot out more and more so when he hits it another wave of pleasure rushes all over my body. I close my eyes as a mini orgasm builds and causes me to squirt. He goes faster and I moan louder because it feels so good. Nothing makes me feel better than having him so deep inside of me. Sometimes I look up at him, sweat dripping in my eyes as it rolls down your head, into your face and down all over me because I make your fat ass keep pumping against my cunt as I use my weirding ways utilizing resistance training against you pushing so hard for you to be up inside of me. That "why can't I come" look blazon across his face.

If he thinks I am most beautiful when he is inside of me then he is more handsome this way because I know I am the only one to give him such expressions of loving exstasy as his sweat drips all over me

OCD

Saturday September 11, 1999

I have my apartment almost perfectly in order. I am about to die. I am so happy. I feel my Obsessive Compulsive Disorder is coming out in full force. I am afraid I am not going to stop. I was up most of the day putting the finishing touches on my apartment. I even have four of the 16X20's of my Russian Gay boys.

I am kind of feeling like a kept woman. Last night after an uneventful night of us doing nothing and me laying around naked all night we decided to bathe. Melissa came in the other day and told me I could put something that attaches to the tub to make it into a shower and I looked at her and scoffed "I like taking baths." I love the sensuousness of sitting in hot hot water and just feel it enveloping my body. Kevin wanted a bubble bath so I added some of the bath stuff I got from Jan the first time I was supposed to graduate. This bath tub does not fit two people very well and all I can dream about these days is having a bath tub that can fit two people.

So... I laid in Kevin's lap for a while and looked up at the slanted ceiling that is painted baby blue with **The Garden of Earthly Delights** there for me to stare at. I get bored and start hitting his face with my tits as I look for the razor to shave his head. He gets his head wet and I get it lathered up and shave it all off with the New Mach

I don't know why... maybe it's because he trusts me enough with a razor to his head I get so turned on. I am very careful not to nick his head this time like I did the last time. I think he likes to tell his friends that I shave him with a razor too. He did tell me, however, that he doesn't talk about how after the third time we saw each other he let me shave his balls.

One of the sad state of affairs for a female ejaculator is that if you aren't careful his pubic hair will rub you like a Brillo pad (which is steel wool), and that can be painful. But I shaved his head and his face last night and when I got back in the water he kept talking about how he wanted to make slow love to me. I giggled like a school girl because he was being so silly and there is a woman in the next apartment that cackles like the Blair Witch when she laughs.

Between her and Kevin saying how he was going to lick every inch of my body I just about died. I got out of the bathtub and got situated here, lighting the pillar candles he bought when I had surgery and watched over me that first night with them blazing through my bursts of consciousness. I lit a Sandlewood incense as well, laid out the towels so my bed wouldn't get drenched and he severed his death penalty with pride. It was such a wonderful thing to feel him in between my legs just going to town.

I came and then he got on top of me and moved his hips up in that little hook he does but really slow and meticulous... I kept my eyes open and let him see me cum as he was filling me up. We moved into many different positions... missionary, me on top (which I am beginning to enjoy a lot more), us standing up. Sometimes he's not the greatest boyfriend and he is such a guy... but when he is inside of me he can be so tender, so sweet, so caring ensuring that my body remains responsive with murmurs and screams and grunts and groans in all the different positions. He hits my G-spot with his perfectly sized cock and it makes me push down so I can squirt. I can gush a little or sometimes I can gush a lot. It just depends on how aroused I am. He went on forever last night and didn't cum so this morning we picked right up again only this time I did not cum and it has put a damper on my day. I cleaned a lot and decided to myself that the next time I have cum I am going to tell him I am done and he can finish himself.

I wonder what life would be like for men if women came like oh so many men I have been with and were left with all the pent up sexual frustration like that. Coming so close...

I had a funky dream that has stayed with me all day. I was in California and I was not going to leave but it ended up being Jenn and I was in Richmond, California and I couldn't get a plane home so I decided to stay. Very odd.

So... I am getting to the point where my underware is folded and my socks are all neat in that thingie Tanya gave me almost a year ago. I even have put my food in order and my table up. I have not spent most of the night naked but at least I can watch Howard Stern now.

OCD

CABRINI GREEN

Monday November 1, 1999

She looked out at the men sitting on the jalopy she knew probably didn't run. Tires black and worn from being bald leaned up against the fence. On her way to her job interview she looked around and felt a cold feeling as the car moved through Cabrini Green.

On the way back she felt a little intimidated and she understood that there was no way anyone would get out of their car in this area. She looked up at the buildings... building like from The Full Monty and some of the knock 'em up and move 'em in shit holes in Moscow.

Such a strange existence. She wondered if the mothers there wanted their babies to grow up and move out. Some people make it out of there... I have heard stories. It seems so weird to think that this is the kind of society people try so hard to be a part of.

I got the most beautiful letter in my box today from a guy I met on the nin message board. He wrote:

On the way out I saw some girls practicing that Mexican stomping dance thing. They had an instructor and they were practicing their moves with traditional clothes and everything. It was beautiful. I caught the eye of one of the women dancing and she gave me a rude look which ruined it. Why can't women accept that they are beautiful? Why is it bad to admire their beauty? I left after that defeat because it was no longer beautiful. if women only understood how much power they have. one look can ruin or make your day.-- brandon

It made her a little sad to realize that women are too protective of themselves. Made her think of the feminine role women in the fifties got to play. Their job was to keep house and take care of people. She thought maybe that is something lacking in today's society.

Perhaps she even yearned to be such a woman.

Sometimes she would fantasize about a life where someone could take care of her and she could stay at home and do whatever. But then she remembered she already had that and she took care of herself. Sometimes with a little help from Andy.

She thought of what she meant to different men. She wondered when it would come to a point in her life when a man would accept that relationships take a very long time to develop and that having relationships with several men was normal.

She wondered if humans could ever accept that that's the way it could be or if these assholes that shove their fucking "morals" down their throats would always prevail. She wondered if she could be that way and she often figured she could be. Just walk through this life loving as many men as she possibly could by sharing her soul and her body. Making broken men feel whole and know that there are such creatures that exist and desire nothing from you but such a deep seeded love in your heart.

She thought it was a tragedy that people couldn't start off a relationship thinking that it might not work but maybe sometime down the road check back in with me and we will see what's going on. She felt that way with several of her lovers. Thinking random thoughts occasionally. 'This one was way too fucked in the head and this one is way too selfish but I could live with some of that' were just a few of her thoughts.

She desired a great man. A man that knew his role. A strong man that fixed her breakfast and did the dishes. Someone thoughtful enough to bring her a freshly bloomed daisy from the side of the road. Someone to write poetry. Someone well rounded.

She found such men around her and she always tried to make it a pleasure to be in her company.

On the other side to his letter, she was one of the women other women forgot to be. Someone that enjoyed cooking. Someone that could put up a fight. Someone your friends would be sooo jealous of the first time they heard her say 'cunt.'

Someone that could laugh at herself and wear a strap-on dildo for Halloween (pic coming soon!)

She knew what power he was talking about in his letter. She realized she had it last year in Europe. She hoped every woman reading this went there alone at least once in their lives... alone... with their skirts hiked for anyone desiring a quick midnight fling.

ANAÏS NIN

Thursday November 18, 1999

"It was a struggle with shadows, a story of not meeting the loved one but long one's self in the other" ~Anaïs Nin, Winter of Artifice.

As I read through what Miss Nin had written in this particular story I felt how many of the truths that I felt in my heart applied to her own life. I wanted to scream for her to run and get away from the man that hurt her so deeply only to realize that there is no escape from the very blood that runs through my own veins.

Issues of abandonment, A loss of so much life because the fantasy of daddy coming to save me would never quite happen. I read many of the words of the woman I desire to surpass with my own writing and saw myself, sitting next to Miss Nin on a couch reliving memories that stung them both even today. It did not matter that she was no longer alive... through her words in which I can still feel her pain. They were both lost little girls trying to find a solution to a problem as complex as man is old.

Why did my daddy hurt me so badly?

I thought of my own father and although I figured out many of the fractures in his psyche that led him to abuse me as a child I could still not get over the damage. I've tried to cut it off only to have it grow back. I tried to kill it only to find myself sitting next to a schizophrenic woman in a mental institution. I tried to confront him but my words, my anger, my deep seeded rage was more powerful than even he could understand. I've tried to understand it as I've looked down at my nephews when they angered me but still there was no way I would allow myself to express such emotions and damage them. I tried to run away only to find that somehow, some way daddy followed me wherever I went. There was no escape from him or his jealousy or his abuse. He would always be a part of me, shaping me into the woman he wanted me to have become through silent comments and inattentive mannerisms.

To forget such things would be a crime against the very person I am at the core of my being. I could no longer deny it and I was no longer ashamed. I tried to remember that he was the one that was fucked up and I was simply a reflection of the abuse and "love" he had filled me with.

I think of him and how he implied I will always be fucked up and that was because I have been the empty vessel which he filled with rage, hate and animosity.

But I wasn't like him. I refuse to hate. I pushed the hate to the far reaches of my heart to allow it to rot off the edges and allow the love that was a part of my true nature pump itself richly through my blood.

I read the first sentence of my journal again. I realize that the closest I'd come to finding anyone that matched my heart was

Zack and that's why that shit the preacher was saying the other day made her cry so much. I refuse to believe that any expression of love is a sin. Hate was the sin, and I knew that for a fact because I spent many years of my life bathing in hatred. I no longer choose to hate anyone. Not even my brother because hatred took too much energy away from my soul, my imagination and my deep seeded desire to be loved as much as she could be loved.

I could still say fuck my brother, but there was no feeling behind the memory for what he had done... only pity because he never came out of his bath of hatred.

Zack had told me there was no evil in hating, but I know that I could hold such a deep hatred for things that it was just easier to expel all hatred. Zack was so incredibly beautiful. The things that made me love him never dissipated but the memories I have for him were filled with love. Even the fight they had that had hurt us both served as a reminder to me that there was nothing to be gained by hurting one another.

I needed him. I needed his guidance and support through all the storms that I am facing. He was good to me and I returned and nurtured the love I carry for him in return. I thought that this was the way most relationships should go but they often fell short. I could also see so much of myself in him.

As an adult, I could emotionally carry on no matter what happened to me but the fractured child that resided inside was inconsolable. I wished many times that I could love myself the way I deserve to be loved so as an adult I wouldn't be so starved for affection and attention.

BATTLE OF THE SEXES

Sunday December 12, 1999

There was milk in the fridge when I got home and he showed up to the airport a little late so that as he was desperately looking at arrivals I was already walking up to him and about to kiss him before he realized I was right in front of him. He handed me the single, red rose and balloon of Elvis. I kept wrapping my arms around him and kissing all over his bald head.

We went to the store to pick up my photos and I saw many interesting photos from the past 4 months that I had not gotten developed. Michael in Chicago... Colleen and her on the cruise... Zack held Colin as he slept.

Then he wanted to take me out to dinner and I told him Arby's was fine with me. I wanted to go home and feel him next to my naked body. I could not believe how much I ached from not having physical contact from him. I was almost as ashamed of having to feel him inside me as I was sure most men felt powerless to women.

It seemed to me that the battle of the sexes was a hoax. The only reason men felt they needed to dominate women was because we caused sensations and feelings in their bodies they could not control much less understand. Pornography was not about objectifying women, I felt, it was more about getting men anestizied to any one woman.

I held the photographs of Keir's naked body in my hand from Amsterdam and almost died. A flood of wonderful memories pervaded my senses of the week we spent in bliss. Oh man... hitting the ceiling cumming so hard. I had no idea such intimate portraits would lead to my vagina would be feeling such overwhelming vaginal memories again. I quivered.

We had chatted on **ICQ** the night before... telling each other some of the things we wanted to do to one another. As soon as everything was out of the car he was on top of me. My body ached for him. I kissed all over him, so appreciative of his love, hungry for his touch and yearning for his intellect. I was slowly allowing myself to feel my love for him.

I talked to her older sister on the phone for almost an hour. Their bond was getting tighter and tighter. She exclaimed "Catherine, Catherine... oh what a life you lead!" and thanked her for being a wonderful aunt. I wanted to cry when I heard these words because it showed me that I was indeed appreciated.

I talked to Granny for a while and then as soon as I hung up he pounced on me like a kitten with a toy. He held me close standing behind me caressing and feeling my soft, milky skin.

I am a girly girl, even though I rarely wore make up or a bra. I told him as we bathed together in the tub how I saw **Bringing**

Out the Dead on Friday night with Sam. Nicholas Cage had this great line... he had been divorced for a while and woke up in Mary's apartment and went to wash his face. "There were three different soaps smelling of different seasons..." I told him how much I enjoyed that part and what he must have thought the first time he saw my toiletries.

Echo said to Sam when they were here "coming to Cathy's is like going to a spa." Which naturally made her feel even more girly.

When he first went inside of me I felt as if my heart stopped. It hurt just a little and I felt once again like being with him was completely different. Kissing, moaning, pumping away my mind was concentrating on the absolutely exstasy he was delivering bit by bit and then full force slow, fast sometimes hard and evenly paced.

I had thought about sin and how as a heathen since I didn't know Christ then how could I possibly be a sinner? And my grandmother told me that when she would sin she would feel guilty but nothing s

I had done something out of the ordinary in my life that made me feel like she was a bad person.

"I love you, Sassy Joe."

"Again."

"I love you, baby."

"Again."

"Uhhh... Aye yay yay."
"Why?"

"Because you are a good person, a good Aunt, you are caring..."

"But how do I make you feel?"

I straddle him and started to give him little kisses on his lips and eyes. I made him hold still as I massaged his eyebrow with my lips and intermittently switched to kisses. I moved my mouth to his closed eyes and tenderly kissed his eyelids. I rubbed my face against his and ticked him with my long hair.

I was very glad to be home.

MONDAY DECEMBER 13, 1999

I sipped the **Marker's** and Coke (all Kanfuckians bleed Bourbon) and thought back to the first time I was ever drunk. I wondered if that memory would live with me forever. I thought of the intermittent times I had drank whiskey and coke and if it brought me much delight. I was an alcoholic, that was part of my DNA since my father's side were all a bunch of lushes. Unless you don't count drinking everyday just-a-little-drink as alcoholism.

There was more liquor on top of our refrigerator than clothes that hung in my closet when I was a child. (As a protest, I kept cereal boxes, oatmeal and pancake mix there now.) Nice, expensive liquor which is where I had taken the **Maker's Mark** from in order to experience this glory drinking was supposed to bring.

I remember being 13 and staggering drunk, scaring my sister to death because Anne had never seen her that way. But then she wondered...

Last night on 2 a.m. **Oprah** I watched as this man talked about addictions as wounds that needed healing. I don't drink on a regular basis but I'm predisposed to being alcoholic. I love sex voraciously, but I had been with only one man for 6 months now. I loved the consolation of food and thought of my own excitement and pleasure I derived from being bulimic. I also wondered if I didn't love milk for the very reason that it brought me so much comfort... and if every time I drank it I was reminded of when my mother gave it to me in a bottle.

Aug 2021

And reading this 20 years later with chipped teeth from the acid eating away at my teeth. Once you have an eating disorder it never really leaves you. You feel the anorexia sleep inside your bones when you realize that you hadn't eaten for days or if you had you didn't know what it was. It was either that are the satisfaction of eating so much food I just to feel like you need **Un Wafier** can pop the Easter can't stop so you fill your pie hole with all your transgressions, aggression, submissives, dismisses, preconceived notion of what life was in store for you instead of what you were in store for life.

So so so much more of those into an eating disorder because it's one that is denying one of the most basic of pleasures and that is to satiate the need to live. The survival of the fittest and you don't have to be so thin anymore which is really something that I never thought I would see on TV. Something called fat equality? Looking at this TV screen it doesn't seem like every girl is going to keep her guts out because she is not eating just so she can be crowd-pleasing.

I'm an almond of death that one shares by themselves. The fingers behind the throat rub uvula as you feel the pieces and your throat that are the cock blocks that some men hit. Controlling something that is in controllable a satiating need to feel call which is something I even Stars love to stand and see how their perfection can be reflected upon thee.

It doesn't matter if it's Mind Over Matter because as long as you mind and everything matters. The things that are in front of you that you have control of are the things that you do and when you feel they are out of control there go your feelings and here comes the roll of your fingers doing something they did in Roman times.

What did they do once their teeth were all eaten? From eating and eating and arfeen is up could you imagine a party where people could do this? I'm sure there'd be money in that.

WHISKEY DICK

There are certain changes my body undergoes when I have been drinking. Kevin calls it whiskey dick only last night I wasn't drinking whiskey but beer. He had a particularly shitty day and both his clients were sent to jail for 20 years. He was not a happy camper.

I was horny as fuck so I called him after midnight and he swore to me he had to wake up early and do all this shit today.

"Sassy Joe, No."

"Then talk dirty to me."

"You mean you want me to tell you what it's like when the big fat cock goes inside and your pussy is hungry for it. Your pussy gets all hot and wet and wraps clamps down on the big fat cock..."

"Well, I might as well come over because now I have a chubby."

We fucked like minx baby, yeah. And then after we were done and we were about to fall asleep I rolled over and began sucking his cock and made him hard again so he could fuck me again. I love fucking Kevin. I don't know if I am in love with him but I do love his cock slamming hard inside of me.

You know what the best orgasms for a woman are? The ones where you tent and you can actually feel your cunt trembling from torrents of pleasure. Those are my favorites anyway. And I can assure you every time I am with Kevin I achieve such orgasms because he usually waits for me to finish first.

I think the most sadistic thing I have ever done to one of my lovers is to tell him he couldn't come even though I already had. ("she's not a slut yet give her time! "). The pained look on his face brought a certain amount of pleasure to me simply because I knew he couldn't come because I told him not to.

Can I tell you how much I love being a girl?

My hands smell like girl cum today. I keep getting wafts of girl cum as I am working even though I have washed my hands. Sometimes that smell never comes off.

SEPERATE BEDROOMS

Granny and Pop went to bed so we sat around and talked and watched **Duckman**. It was a very good night. We talked about some stuff and laid around and rubbed on each other. I told him he couldn't touch me in my chest or down my pants because you never know when my grandparents might have to get up and pee.

He didn't like that. So when he got real frisky I went and took a bath. Ahhh a bathtub that is warm with warm water... kind of. Oh how I long to have a bath tub with endless vats of hot steamy water.

Then we went into my old bedroom and kissed for a while until he wouldn't kiss me anymore because his mustache is too long and it felt weird. I rolled over and was in that stage between just falling asleep and being asleep when I thought I heard one of the strangest noises I have ever heard. Was someone using that bathroom? Was this place being haunted? I shot out of bed and started calling for Kevin. I went to where he was and he wasn't there. I started freaking out and then I realized he was taking a leak and that's what I heard.

I made him lay with me for a second and then he went to sleep in his own bed. It was a nice change of pace.

We woke up and had oatmeal and then went shopping.

We got back to the house and had country fried steak and gravy and then we all went and looked at the property my grandfather owns. We went to **Penn's Store** as well. It's the oldest store from back in the day and I mean back in the 1700s or something like that. We rode in Pop's caddy. It's such a pimp mobile. Gray exterior and maroon interior. It was a nice drive and seeing nature was also soothing.

Leaving one the other hand… things haven't been right since Granny and Pop saw my photos of my Russian gay boys. "I love you Poppa."

"IF YEW LOVED ME you'd take those photos of yours and just throw them in the garbage dump."

Just shut up Pop. "You know what the bible says about that?"

Yada yada yada. I left pissed and I don't like that.

I thought of all kinds of stories to write about. Stories I should write about like what it was like to be in Spain. Other more interesting things but now I am tired and it's late… tomorrow… I can write more tomorrow.

THIN VOLUME 1

ABOUT THE AUTHOR

My name is Catherine Elizabeth Clay. My mother, Patsy Waits Clay, said she named me for 2 queens. My family is THE family that has spun the US into the Mafia powerhouse it is today. Since 1613.

I became Catherine the Great, Impress of the internet, after being bullied by a computer engineer internet millennia ago in 1992. I became "Egotistical Site Of the Week" calling myself OneOpinionatedBitch.Com.

I am one of the most hidden influencers on the internet because I wrote the first article on female ejaculation, "The Gentle Art of Female Ejaculation AKA How to Fuck Like a Porn Star" OneOpinionatedBitch.Com/I/love/sex for "The Post Feminist Playground" in 1997 so these hands have been in billions of pussy.

PurePhotography.Com is the oldest photography website as well as DearDementedDiary.Com being the oldest online diary.

I started writing when I was 9 and won 2nd place for creative writing in 4th and 5th grades.

These first III Volumes of "101 Shades of Clay" are inspired by one of the loves of my life, Joshua Harris. I was born on Marilyn Monroe's birthday so I believe there are several souls to be mated to and monogamy, although a nice thought, is antiquated as my 50 year old ass.

Please enter marriage KNOWING there's always someone else to fly by. Just come home to Daddy.

I live in Los Angeles and have a teenage son. I'm pretty isolated, introverted and insecure so please keep our contact to events meant to be celebrated. I'd love to keep writing for you so be mindful of my very limited neurodivergent mind space. I write what I know and my art speaks for itself. The knowledge you garner will hopefully blow your neurotypical mind.

I live with a brain tumor you get the age with, an arachnoid cyst or a pocket of goo they have a hard time to remove. It's caused Chiari, EDS, MS and Syringomyelia just to name a few CNS diseases.

www.ingramcontent.com/pod-product-compliance
Lightning Source LLC
Chambersburg PA
CBHW041048310726
48978CB00011BA/473